About the

Brandon Robshaw is the author of 26 children's novels and over 60 educational books. His most recent children's novel, *The Big Wish*, was published by Chicken House in 2015. It was shortlisted for the James Reckitt Hull Children's Book Award 2016. His collection of children's poetry, *These Are a Few of my Scariest Things,* was published in 2017 by the King's England Press.

Brandon is also a freelance journalist and used to be a regular book reviewer for the *Independent on Sunday.* He lectures in Creative Writing, Children's Literature, and Philosophy for the Open University, and Writing for Children for Westminster University and St Mary's University; he has a degree in English Literature and an MA in Philosophy, and is currently studying for a PhD in Philosophy with the Open University. He enjoys running, plays the ukulele a little bit and the piano an even littler bit. He blogs about the state of the English language from a liberal pedant's perspective.

Brandon may also be familiar as the dad in the BBC television programme *Back in Time for Dinner*, a 6-part series about the history of food in Britain from the 1950s to the present-day. The first series was shown in 2015 on BBC2. The follow-up series, *Back in Time for Christmas*, went out in December 2015 and has since been repeated every Christmas. The latest series, *Further Back in Time*, was in 2017.

brandonrobshaw.wordpress.com
@BrandonRobshaw

THE INFINITE POWERS OF ADAM GOWERS

THE INFINITE POWERS OF ADAM GOWERS

BRANDON ROBSHAW

This edition first published in 2018

Unbound

6th Floor Mutual House, 70 Conduit Street, London W1S 2GF

www.unbound.com

ISBN (eBook): 978-1-912618-35-4

ISBN (Paperback): 978-1-912618-34-7

Design by Designer

Printed in Great Britain by Clays Ltd, Elcograf S.p.A

Dear Reader,

The book you are holding came about in a rather different way to most others. It was funded directly by readers through a new website: Unbound.

Unbound is the creation of three writers. We started the company because we believed there had to be a better deal for both writers and readers. On the Unbound website, authors share the ideas for the books they want to write directly with readers. If enough of you support the book by pledging for it in advance, we produce a beautifully bound special subscribers' edition and distribute a regular edition and e-book wherever books are sold, in shops and online.

This new way of publishing is actually a very old idea (Samuel Johnson funded his dictionary this way). We're just using the internet to build each writer a network of patrons. Here, at the back of this book, you'll find the names of all the people who made it happen.

Publishing in this way means readers are no longer just passive consumers of the books they buy, and authors are free to write the books they really want. They get a much fairer return too – half the profits their books generate, rather than a tiny percentage of the cover price.

If you're not yet a subscriber, we hope that you'll want to join our publishing revolution and have your name listed in one of our books in the future. To get you started, here is a £5 discount on your first pledge. Just visit unbound.com, make your pledge and type GOWERS18 in the promo code box when you check out.

Thank you for your support,
unbound-signatures-for-letter

Dan, Justin and John
    Founders, Unbound

Super Patrons

Bilal Abdullah
David Alterman
Maria Anastasi
Bridget Anderson
Mary Archer
Sam Ardley
Will Ashon
Jason Ashwood
Susie Attwood
Alethea Baker
Judith Barrett
Veronika Binoeder
David Birch
Hannah Bird
sue bloomfield
Nick Boughton
Steve Bowerman
Mark Brafield
Karen Brown
Claire Brown
Aisling Browne
Marnie Buchanan
Peter Buchanan
Christine Burns
Tom Carradine
Simon Carter
Avirup Chaudhuri
Joe Chislett
Laura Clark
Nicholas Clarke
Alan Cohen
Nicky Cook

Anto Cooper
Giles Coren
John Crawford
John Cretton
Christine Dale
John Dale
Peter Dann
Rob Davidson
Russell Delew
Penny Demetriou
Bruce Dessau
Teresa Dicken
Sue Dodd
Ben Eagle
Deb Edmunds
Laura Ellings
Sarah Farley
Diane Featherstone
Charlie Finlay
Ruth Fischelis
Nathan Fox
Matthew Frost
Sarah & Andy G
Lynn Gard
Jonathan Gibbs
Lucy Gibson
Alison Gillow
David Gillow
Harold Gillow
Eleanor Glover
Adelaide Glover
David Glover
Bronwen Glover
Owen Glover
Douglas Googe
Suzanbe Gowers

Martin Gray
Suzanne Grundy
Katy Guest
Paul Gunning
Charlotte Hall
Jayne Harrill
Andrea Hart
Mirjam Hauck
Rob Hawkins
Ethan Hodgkinson
Peter Howell
Mick Hume
Stephen James
Angela James, children's author
Fuzzy Jones
Mike Katholnig
Rachel Kellett
Dan Kelly
Dan Kieran
Sarah Kiernan
Janet Kirkwood
Lukas Kuhn
Pierre L'Allier
Gary Lancet
Peter Lawson
Rob Lemkin
Ishraga Lloyd
Margaret Lucille Kekewich
James Lyons
Kim Maddever
Oliver Mason
Derek Matravers
Isabel May
Tom McLaughlin
John Mitchinson
David Moloney

Lynne Moore
Mark Morfett
Dan Muirden
Stephen Murgatroyd
Paul Oakley
Simon Odell
Gerard Omasta-Milsom
Bob Owens
Sarah Palmer
Sarah Pawlett Jackson
Jon Pike
Justin Pollard
Christine Poutney
Jane Purcell
Phyllis Ramage
Alison Ramsey
Debbie Raw
Anne Redmond
Barry Rees
Sarah Richmond
Alec Rivers
Carys Robshaw
Glynis Robshaw
Rochelle Robshaw
Lia Ryan
Lucy Schofield
Martin Scholar
Evelyn Scholar
Joanna Sephton
Kate Smith
Chris Snowdon
Duncan Stingemore
Ashley Stokes
Rebekah Sutherland
Susie Swift
Vinay Talwar

Tot Taylor
Dylan Thomas Robinson
Annie Tomkins
Townsend-Elliotts
Steven Trythall
David Tubby
Terry Vass
Neil Vickers
Jessica Voorsanger
Naomi Warren
Paul Watson
Sue Wheat
Joe Worrall
Ed Wright
Naoko Yamagata

PART ONE: HOW IT ALL BEGAN

CHAPTER 1

I'll never forget the day I met the genie and he granted me an infinite number of wishes. Infinite, yeah, that's right. Kind of hard to get your head round, isn't it? I remember Mr David G. Tubby going on about it in maths once, when I was actually listening for a change. He said you can never reach infinity, cause if you take the biggest number you can think of you can always add one to it. Then you can always add one to that. And to that. You can add ten, add a million, double it, times it by itself, keep doing that for a billion trillion years and you still won't have got anywhere near infinity. Infinity isn't the sort of thing you *can* get near.

And that's how many wishes I've got. An infinite number. It's a lot of wishes. Made a big difference to my life, I can tell you. And to yours too. But you won't know about that.

Funny to think if I hadn't gone up in the attic that day – or if I'd gone up there and not noticed the lamp – none of this stuff would ever have happened. But I just happened to catch a glimpse of this lamp, right, in the beam of the torch from my phone. It was half-hidden under an old rug and a portrait of a sad-looking babe with a harp. So I picked it up and blew the dust off and had a look. It was made of bronze or brass or copper or something – one of those old-fashioned oil lamps with a spout, the sort Aladdin has in the pantomime.

Course, I didn't think of Aladdin at the time. I wasn't really expecting a genie to come out and grant me a shedload of wishes. I was thinking of the 'Antiques Roadshow', you know? (Not my favourite show, but my mum watches it and sometimes I've sat through it with her when there's nothing else to do on a Sunday evening.) The lamp looked old and kind of Eastern, just the sort of thing that guy with the moustache, the one my mum likes, would purr over and ask if it had ever been valued. And I'd go, 'Nah', casual-like, as if it was the last thing on my mind, and then, after a long tantalising pause, the guy would be like, 'I think this would fetch ten thousand pounds at auction,' and I'd act cool like they always do and I'd be like, 'Oh, really, I had no idea,' and then the minute the camera was off me I'd be jumping up and down punching the air and I'd be like, 'Yesss!!!'

The funny thing is, I wasn't even looking for a lamp. I'd only gone up in the attic to look for my dad's old tennis racket. I'm not that interested in tennis, to be honest. I reckon it's a silly game, all that fifteen–love stuff – I mean, what's that all about, fifteen–love? Why can't they just say one–nil? Give me football any day. But I needed a tennis racket because…

Wait a minute. I've started in the wrong place here. To explain about the tennis racket I'll have to explain about Natalie – and that all started, really, from a conversation I had with Dirk one day. Yeah, I'll go back to that. Dirk and Natalie are both going to figure in this story a lot, so let's start with them.

OK.

Once upon a time, I was walking to school with my mate Dirk, swinging my Adidas bag with my football kit in. It was a bright, sunny Friday in early February, the kind of day that makes you think spring's nearly here, but you can't really relax and enjoy it because it's still winter, the trees are still bare and any moment an icy gale could come sweeping in and freeze your bollocks off. If you'll pardon my French.

I did at least have a warm coat to guard against unexpected north winds. It was a duffle coat my mum had bought in the January sales. I wasn't any too sure about that coat. I shouldn't complain because I was with her and I did actually choose it. At least I said OK when she pointed it out. Not that there was a huge amount of choice because she said she only had fifty squid to spend. It was black with a tartan lining and wooden toggles. I thought it would be a little bit different, a little bit quirky, you know. Sort of a bit Bohemian. But since I'd started wearing it to school it had attracted some what you might term vulgar commentary.

So, anyway, we're having one of those conversations, Dirk and me. He's doing Philosophy AS, and they'd been doing some stuff about what the purpose of life is or some crap like that, and now he was telling me all about it. I'm not doing Philosophy, by the way. I'm doing English, Economics and History. And French, which I'm fairly *merde* at and will almost certainly have to drop at the end of the year. Unless I drop Economics. I'm not too hot at that one, either.

Anyway, so Dirk was like, 'Spose there was this machine, right, called an Experience Machine – and you could get in it and you'd be in a, like, trance, and it would make you completely happy, cause it'd make you think you were having all the experiences you wanted.'

'OK, spose there was.'

'And spose you could spend your whole life in it, right, it would be just like a fantastic dream that lasted seventy years or whatever, only you wouldn't know it was a dream, you'd think all the stuff you wanted to happen was really happening.'

'Right.'

'Well, would you get in it?'

I was like, 'Course I'd get in it. A lifetime of getting everything you wanted? Who'd turn that down?'

'Yeah, but it wouldn't be real. You'd just be sitting in a machine.'

'Yeah, but once you were in, you'd think it was real. You could make all your wishes come true!'

'It would only *seem* like they'd come true.'

'That's good enough for me.'

Dirk was like, 'What would you wish for, then? Hold on, lemme guess. You'd wish for a new coat, right?'

I gave him a shove. 'Piss off! This is a good coat, this is. It's a classic.'

'Yeah, a classic piece of crap.'

Dirk was wearing a parka. That was a safe bet. Nearly all the kids had parkas. My duffle coat was out on its own.

'Well, I tell you something, I wouldn't wish for a *parka* if I was in the Experience Machine. I wouldn't wish to be exactly the same as everyone else, I can tell you that.'

'What would you wish for, then? Hold on, lemme guess... you'd be a Premier League footballer, right? And you'd drive a Porsche or a Lamborghini or some shit like that. And you'd travel to outer space for your holidays.'

He knows me pretty well, Dirk. We've known each other since we were really little kids. We were at nursery together. And his mum used to look after me after school when we were at primary school and my mum was working in John Lewis. She used to give us alphabetti spaghetti on toast and me and Dirk used to arrange it into rude words when her back was turned.

Anyway I felt a bit annoyed because he'd basically just reeled off my wish-list. And I wanted to come up with something unexpected, a wish he hadn't predicted that would surprise him.

And when it came out it surprised me too.

I was like, 'If I was in the Experience Machine, I'd go out with Natalie Forbes.'

Dirk stopped walking and looked at me. I stopped walking and looked at him back.

Natalie Forbes is – well, she's not what you'd call a babe. She's clever, a bit of a boffin, she got a whole bunch of A-stars in her GCSEs and she'll pick up another bunch in her AS levels. She wears small square black glasses and has short straight black hair. She's not bad-looking, she's quite OK in a dark, quiet sort of way, but she hasn't got that sort of upfront sexiness some girls have, the ones who are well-known for being babes, you know. And at this time I didn't even know her all that well. Or at least, I did in a way, cause we'd been at the same school for nearly six years, and over that time you get a general idea of what someone's like. And we'd say 'Hi' and pass the time of day, and we were friends on Facebook and we had each other's contact details on our phones – but that didn't mean anything cause nearly everyone in the year was friends on Facebook and had each other's contact details. The point I'm trying to get at is that we weren't close friends and I'd probably spent in total no more than a few minutes thinking about her in my whole life. So like I say, I was surprised when I realised how much I fancied her.

But it was the sort of surprise you feel when you've just realised something that in a way you knew all along, and you wonder why it took so long to see it.

Dirk raises his eyebrows in this sort of quizzical way he has (I reckon he practises in front of the mirror). 'Really? You fancy Natalie Forbes?'

'She's all right. Wouldn't say no, you know what I mean.'

'Yeah.' Dirk nods now, thinking about it. 'Yeah, she's all right.'

For some reason, even though he's agreeing with me, I feel annoyed. Who does he think he is, to judge and grade Natalie like that? Plus, I sort of liked the idea that only I could see how sexy Natalie was, like there was something special about me that was able to pick out what was special about her. It seemed to show that we were meant for each other. I didn't want other guys fancying her. So I didn't want to get in a debate with Dirk about how attractive Natalie was.

I was like, 'Well, anyway, that's what I'd wish for. What about you, what would you wish for?'

'Nothing, cause I wouldn't get in the machine. I prefer reality.'

'Reality's rubbish, man. Reality is so unspeakably sordid it makes me shudder.'

Dirk laughed. I've found that's quite a good way to make people laugh, to throw in a burst of unexpected vocabulary. Actually I was cheating a bit because I'd nicked that line out of one of my dad's old kids' books he once gave me to read when I was younger. About a kid called Molesworth. It sort of stuck in my mind.

The street was getting crowded now, black with kids in uniforms streaming into school. We went in through the gates just as the bell was ringing.

'Hey Adam! Still wearing that coat?'

'He don't give up easy.'

'Persistent!'

These annoying comments came from Maxwell Ramage, Ibrahim Wahed and Spencer Spragg. They weren't enemies of mine. They were just having a laugh, trying to enliven proceedings while we were lining up – well, sort of seething around – outside the form-room for registration, waiting for Miss Barrowmere to come and unlock the door.

I was like, 'Coats like this are the latest thing. Stormzy wears one. He sent me a picture on Instagram.'

Another way of getting a laugh is to make some crazy, unbelievable claim. It's not bragging, because no one's supposed to believe it. It usually works, if the lie is outrageous enough and you come out with it fast enough. On this occasion it got a good laugh. Max, Ibrahim and Spence sort of chuckled in a kind of OK-give-you-that-one kind of way. Dirk laughed, so did Martin Bone. I glanced across to where Natalie was standing with her friends Claire and Shushmita. Shushmita was smiling a bit. Claire laughed properly, with her mouth wide open. But Natalie wasn't laughing. Her face was completely unsmiling. She looked like some sort of noble, dignified beautiful statue with glasses on.

That was not the best sign. You can always tell if people like you by if they laugh at your jokes.

Everyone's got something, you know? Some sort of skill or quality that gives them a certain amount of status. Like, Martin Bone's good at football. Really good. (Actually he's good at all sports.) Dirk, like Natalie, is a brainbox. But more than that, he's kind of... *cool*, in the sense that he always seems to say the right thing. Never puts a foot wrong. Never embarrasses himself.

Now, I'm not specially good at anything. (Or specially bad, either, to be fair.) The main thing I have going for me is that I can make people laugh. Sometimes. Not all the time. But my hit-rate isn't too bad. It's not much, but it's all I've got.

I made a vow to myself that I'd make Natalie laugh before the end of the day. Somehow.

'Morning everyone!'

Miss Barrowmere had arrived.

'But perhaps Adam can enlighten us?'

'What?'

It was first period. Economics. Mr Tubby had started off explaining how important probability theory was in classical economics because without it people couldn't make rational choices. After that it got a bit mathematical and I zoned out. Tubby used to take me for maths. I was never all that great at maths and only just scraped through the GCSE. I was thankful to see the back of it, and of Tubby – only to find I still had him for Economics. And the subject turned out to have more maths in it than I'd bargained for. Out of the mathematical frying pan into the economic fire, sort of thing. Tubby had been droning on and covering the whiteboard with calculations for the last ten minutes, but I'd hardly heard a word. I'd been staring out of the window thinking about Natalie. She was sitting just a couple of places behind me and I liked the idea that she'd be able to see the back of my head.

Tubby was like, 'What was I saying just now?'

'Er – something about a hat, wasn't it?'

'Something about a hat. I see.' There were a few sniggers round the classroom. People were sitting up and taking notice, now. Tubby was about to launch into one of his famous sarcasm routines, and I was going to be the victim. 'Something about a hat. I've just spent ten minutes explaining the intricacies of probability theory and Adam here has succeeded in grasping the essential point that it's something to do with hats.' He paused for the laugh, and got it, big-time. 'But I'm sure Adam here has other things on his mind – more pressing matters – affairs of greater importance and urgency. Perhaps you'd like to tell us what you were thinking about, Adam?'

'Nothing.'

'Nothing. I see. "Nothing" is a subject you find absorbing, is it?'

I squeezed my brain to see if I could think of some witty retort – something to get the class laughing and on my side. But my brain was dry. All I could manage was, 'Not really.'

'Not really. I see. Well, perhaps you could focus your enormous mental powers on the subject of something, rather than nothing, for a moment. Could you do that for me? Please?'

'OK.'

'Good, good. Now, this hat of which you were speaking. It's got raffle tickets in it, hasn't it?'

'Er... yeah.'

'Now, these raffle tickets are different colours, aren't they? Ten are green and twenty are red. That's right, isn't it? So, if I dip my hand in and take two tickets out, without looking, what would you say is the probability that I would have one of each colour?'

'Er... well... to be honest, I haven't a clue.'

'Is the right answer! I couldn't have put it better myself. You haven't a clue.'

This brought the house down, of course. Tubby smirked, well pleased with himself. He gets a kick out of being sarcastic. He doesn't do it to everyone – he wouldn't dare try it on the real troublemakers, the hard cases like Steve Renwick. But I'm one of his favourite targets. I don't know why. Cause there's no reason to be scared of me, I suppose.

And of course, I am crap at anything to do with maths. I don't even know why I took Economics. Well, I do, actually. The truth is I only took it because there weren't enough subjects I'd done well in at GCSE.

'Well, well, let's try someone who might have a clue. Natalie?'

I squirmed round in my seat to watch her serious, sweetly conscientious face as she considered the problem, explained it and gave the correct answer.

I almost clapped.

I was mooching round with Dirk at break time, thinking about the next double period, i.e. double football. I was hoping I could play well enough to impress Mr Nossiter and get picked for the school team at long, long last – an ambition I'd cherished ever since Year 7. I'm not bad at football at all. Actually, scratch that, I am pretty bad. But I'm not *totally* crap. I'm not the worst in the school. I'd say I'm about, maybe... the thirtieth best player in the year.

Too bad there's only eleven players in a team.

But this week there was a glimmer of a chance. A couple of the regular players – Earl Staunton and Kane Jessamides – were off sick with flu and we had a game this weekend. And of the others who might technically be ahead of me in the queue to replace them, there were bound to be quite a few who weren't free on Saturday or who just weren't interested. No one else was as keen as me. As enthusiastic. If only I could get Nossiter to see that...

'What do you reckon? He's gotta pick me, hasn't he, with Earl and Kane away?'

'Well, maybe, if everyone else plays really shit.'

That wasn't exactly what I wanted to hear. Dirk wasn't in competition with me because he doesn't play football any more. In Year 12, PE isn't on the timetable any more, unless you're doing the AS. You just do sport, if you want to, when you happen to have a free period. So Dirk gave it up. This is typical Dirk, by the way. He was pretty feeble at football, worse than me, and that's why he stopped. He doesn't like to show himself up, he only likes doing things he's good at. Anyway the point is he wasn't my rival for a team place so I didn't see why he couldn't have boosted my chances a bit. *Go for it, I know you can do it, mate* – that sort of thing. But Dirk would never say he knew anything if he didn't. He prides himself on telling it like it is. Or like he thinks it is.

But the next moment all thoughts of football were driven from my mind, because we rounded a corner and guess who should be standing there but...

have a guess...

that's right.

Natalie.

My heart did that sort of somersault you get when you miss your footing at the top of the stairs and think you're going to fall all the way down. She was standing there chatting with Claire and Shushmita. They all looked extra lively and girly, you know the sort of thing, lots of hand movements, loads of expressions flitting over their faces, sudden smiles and giggles, flicking their hair back and all that stuff. I wondered what they were talking about. I felt like I'd never seen girls before. They all looked great – but Natalie looked the best. She'd parked her bag on the ground between her feet and there was a tennis racket sticking out of it. I noticed she was wearing black tights. Nothing special about that – she wore them every day – but today I just thought, 'Wow! Black tights!'

Dirk's like, 'Now's your chance.'

I'm like, 'Shut up,' out the corner of my mouth, and then I go, 'Hey, Natalie!'

'Hi, Adam.'

It gave me a kind of little thrill to hear her say it. She's got a nice voice, quite low, quite posh, and friendly, and she's using it to say *my* name.

Claire was like, 'Hi!'

I nodded vaguely at her and at Shushmita. I was like, 'Er, well, yeah, so Natalie…'

'Yes?'

'Er… you really nailed that question of Tubby's. He asked it, you answered it. Bang! It was like he'd bowled you a fast ball and you slogged it out of the ground! Like in cricket, you know.'

The girls all laugh. Not with any great hilarity. More a sort of polite laugh. Next to me I was aware of Dirk laughing too, but in a slightly different way.

There was a bit of a pause.

I was like, 'Right, yeah, cool.' For the second time that day I squeezed my brain to try and get a witty remark out of it. For the second time the substandard piece of junk let me down. I was like, 'Yeah, cool, right,' and then, 'Cool, right, yeah,' and finally, 'Catch you later, then.'

Dirk was like, 'For another scintillating conversation.'

The girls laugh, with a bit more feeling this time. Including Natalie. I can feel a hot bubbly blush spreading over my face. I turn and walk away. I can feel myself walking stiffly, swinging my arms like a marching soldier, going left-right, left-right.

'You're blushing,' Dirk goes. 'You look like a tomato.'

'Oh, do I? Well, you look like…' (I run a quick mental search for some insulting-sounding fruit or veg) '… an uggli fruit. And what's more, you look like that all the time.' *Now,* of course, now it was too late, the gift of repartee had returned to me.

Dirk goes, 'Oh, *touché.*' He knows a lot of flash words like that. He's another one who'll get a whole bunch of A-stars in his AS's.

'Is she watching me?'

Dirk glances over his shoulder. 'Nah.'

I don't know whether to feel glad or disappointed about this. 'What did you have to show me up like that for, anyway?'

'I was only having a laugh.'

'Yeah, at my expense.'

'Sorry. Couldn't resist.'

I decided to leave it. There's no point bearing a grudge. That's what friends are for, isn't it? To take the piss out of you.

I was like, 'What do you think, anyway?'

'About what?'

'You know. Does she fancy me?'

'I dunno.'

'But didn't you think she said hi in a nice way?'

'Just a normal sort of way, I thought.'

'But she sort of smiled at me, didn't she?'

'I spose.' Dirk looks at me with his quizzical face again. 'You've got it bad, haven't you?'

'Yeah, I have.' The funny thing is, I feel a kind of pride in this confession. 'I've got it really bad.'

'To me!'

I stuck my hand up, waving frantically. Martin Bone was in possession on the left wing. I was on the edge of the penalty area, in a bit of space with a sight of goal – if the ball came to me now the next stop would be the back of the net.

Martin and me go way back. He's the best footballer in the year. In Years 12 and 13 in fact. The school team's star player. He looks like a slightly smaller edition of Jermaine Defoe. He's not tall but he's quick and strongly put together, with a low centre of gravity and great balance. You just can't knock him off the ball. Ever since we used to play together in primary school he's been streets ahead of anyone else. He knows about my ambition to get into the school team. In fact, for a while he used to coach me after school over at the park, practising dribbling and tackling and shooting. Maybe it made me better, I don't know. The trouble was that everyone else was getting better at the same time.

'Hi, Martin! Here!' I waved my hand so hard it hurt.

Martin looked up, feinted to go past his man and in the yard of space he'd created, knocked the ball sweetly across to me.

A defender was running in to close me down. But I had the vital half-second I needed. I drew back my foot –

and booted the ball –

about seven metres over the crossbar.

There was a kind of chorus of moans and weary sighs from my team. Martin put his hands on his hips and looked at me. I made what you might call a helpless gesture of apology.

Mr Nossiter blew his whistle. 'All right, go and get it, Gowers.'

As I jogged over the field to retrieve the ball, two words kept repeating themselves in my head. And one rhymed with *fit* and the other rhymed with *duck*.

I reckon there should be a limit to how much humiliation a person suffers in any one day. Like, if you've been humiliated once, that should be it – you should be excused any more humiliation for the rest of the day. But that's not how it works. There was more to come.

I was standing in the lunch queue with Dirk, wondering whether to have vegetarian Thai curry or meatballs and pasta (no contest if only it had been Thai meatball curry and rice, but there you go) when Steve Renwick came barging in and pushed in front of us. Now, normally I wouldn't argue about this. You don't argue with Steve Renwick. He's the terror of Year 12. A nutter. A head case. A psycho. He's not just a big kid who likes throwing his weight around. He's a street-fighter, a warrior – fighting's a way of life to him, not messing-about pretend fighting but the real stuff, kick-him-in-the-balls, gouge-him-in-the-eye, smash-him-on-the-head-with-a-bottle kind of fighting. After a fight with him, you'd need a blood transfusion.

That's why what I did next was so insane. But I was having a hard day. I'd been made to look a complete birdbrain in Economics and then got all tongue-tied in front of Natalie and then totally ballsed up my chance to impress Nossiter on the football field. I'd just about had enough, you know? And Renwick had shoved me hard. Before I could stop myself I'd blurted out a protest.

'Hey – you can't barge in like that, man!'

Renwick's like, 'I just did.'

He gave me his thousand-yard stare. I knew what the stare meant, obviously. It meant, just shut up and back down and there'll be no trouble. Cause the funny thing about Renwick is, he's not exactly a bully in the traditional sense of the word. He doesn't pick on people who don't want to fight. That'd be against his warrior's code. He only fights people who are up for it, people who don't mind risking their necks against him. And let's face it, he wouldn't get much glory from beating *me* up.

So the wise thing would have been to just shut up and back down. But Natalie was nearby. I knew she could hear all this. I'd already done my best to impersonate a moron today – I didn't want to show her that I was a wimp as well. I wanted to prove to her that I wasn't afraid of Renwick. Even though, obviously, I was.

So I was like, 'There's a queue, Renwick.'

Renwick eyeballed me again, without saying anything for a bit. Then he was like, 'You disrespecting me, man?'

This was totally unfair. I was like, 'No, *you* were disrespecting *me*.'

Renwick's eyes narrowed. He moved closer to me. I could smell the stale tobacco on his breath. 'What you gonna do about it, then? Gonna meet me on the waste ground after school?'

I was like, 'I can't. I got my piano lesson tonight.'

There was a burst of laughter from the onlookers. It must have been the wimpiest excuse for dodging out of a fight they'd ever heard. Renwick laughed too. Then he stepped into the queue in front of me and turned his back.

That should have been that, really. I should have left it there. But it was one humiliation too many for me. I'd just had enough. So this is where I completely lost the plot.

I tapped Renwick on the shoulder. 'Meet you there on Monday, though.'

Everyone goes quiet. Dirk's looking at me as if I've gone totally insane. Claire's mouth is wide open in a kind of comic-book expression of shock and horror. Natalie's looking at me, too, but I can't work out what her expression means. As if I was some kind of interesting specimen, or an animal behaving strangely in its enclosure in the zoo.

'Right,' goes Renwick. 'Better phone an undertaker.'

'What you gonna do, man? He'll kill you!'

'Oh, well, thanks a bunch, Dirk. That really cheers me up.'

We were walking home. All afternoon, nobody at school had talked about anything else except my fight with Renwick. ('Have you heard the news? Adam's gonna fight Renwick on the waste ground after school on Monday!' 'What? Adam *Gowers?*') Nobody could believe it. Cause there was hardly anybody in the school who'd dream of having a crack at Renwick. Maybe Desmond Jesmond might have fancied his chances, but that was about it. And as for me, I'd never been in a proper fight since I'd been at the school. It's just not my thing. Not my cup of tea. So picking Renwick to start on – well, let's say it was a tad ambitious.

'Still, I gotta say, yo, respect!'

'Respect? It'll be more like last respects.'

Dirk laughed. Not a belly laugh, just a sort of acknowledgment that I'd said something funny, or, if not exactly funny, kind of in the vicinity of being funny. I felt cheered up, just for a second or two, by the success of my crap joke.

'You're living proof of Freud's theory of the Thanatos drive, you are.'

'What are you chatting about? Spikka da Eengleesh?'

'Freud said everyone's got a death wish. Part of you is, like, attracted to the idea of being killed.'

'Oh, is that right?'

He's full of crap like this, Dirk. He comes from a kind of intellectual family.

'How was your day at school?'

'All right.' It's a sketchy description of a day when I fell in love, got made to look a complete idiot and signed my own death warrant. But they're not the kinds of things you tell your mum, really. Not in my family, anyway.

'How was your piano lesson?'

'It was OK.'

This was an out-and-out lie. I hadn't practised all week and by the time I'd stumbled halfway through 'The Trout' Yvonne was begging to me to stop. She said there wasn't much point in continuing the lessons if I wasn't prepared to practise. I don't know why I started them, really. Well, I do. I thought I might get to play keyboard in a band if I learned the piano. But being able to play the first half of 'The Trout' really badly isn't much of a qualification for being in a band.

Bobbligrubs came shambling up and started snuffling round my trousers. He could probably smell Yvonne's Yorkshire terrier on me. She'd jumped on my lap when I sat down to play the piano. The Yorkshire terrier had, I mean, not Yvonne. The lesson wasn't that exciting. I pushed Bobbligrubs away. He's a nice dog, but kind of annoying sometimes. He's got absolutely no sense of personal space.

Emily goes, 'Allo Adam!'

She was sitting on the floor, playing with the cardboard tube out of the inside of a toilet roll. It's her favourite toy. She's got a Playmobil and a pull-along wooden duck and a cuddly Minion and a Fisher Price activity centre and a musical box that plays the 'Teddy Bears' Picnic', but give her a cardboard tube from out of the inside of a toilet roll and she's happy for hours.

I picked her up and sat her on my knee. She laughed and tried to pull my nose. There's a big age gap between us – like, fourteen-and-a-half years – but I get on well with my little sister. She pulled her socks off and started wiggling her toes at me.

'Do "Dis Little Piggy"!'

'All right, then. This little piggy went to market... this little piggy stayed at home...'

Soon she was screaming with laughter. It's easy to make little kids laugh. The simplest thing makes them happy. That's why they're such fun to play with.

'Don't get her overexcited!' my mum goes. I could see she was in one of her moods.

'All right, I was only playing.'

'Yes, well, you play with her and get her all overexcited and then she won't eat her supper and she won't go to sleep – and it's me who has to deal with it, of course, isn't it? It's always me. Not you, not your father. You don't know how wearing it is.'

'Where is Dad, anyway?'

'Your father's out.'

'Where?'

Mum was like, 'He's working!' She sounded kind of snippy, kind of snappy about it. She'd rather have said he was down the pub or something. Something she could blame him for.

Dad's a driving instructor. He hasn't always been one. He used to have a shop. It was a comic-book shop. Classic and vintage comics, graphic novels, collector's editions, all that. But trade dwindled year on year – people don't read comics so much any more, and when they do they buy them online anyway. Plus the rent got put up. In the end he went bust and had to sell all his stock on the internet at rock-bottom prices, which only just raised enough to cover his debts. So Dad started getting work as a driver, because the car was just about the only asset he still had, and while he was doing that he trained as an instructor. And Mum upped her hours at John Lewis.

And then Emily came along.

Mum had to give up her job at John Lewis. For a while there was very little money in our house. When Emily was a little bit older Mum got a part-time job as a librarian, and Dad had to arrange his instructing hours around that. Both time and money were still pretty precarious, though.

I go, 'Would you like a cup of tea?' Might cheer her up a bit, you never know.

She looked at her watch. It was half past five. 'No, I think I might have a drink now. Just a livener, you know.' She went over to the fridge and poured herself a big glass of white wine. 'What are you looking at me like that for?'

'I wasn't looking at you like anything.'

'Weren't you?'

'No.'

She sat down again and took a long pull at her drink. 'Sorry, Adam. I've just had such a hard day. Very wearing.'

'Yeah, me too.'

We heard the key turning in the front door and my dad came in. Bobbligrubs jumped up and ran to greet him. So did Emily.

'You've started early,' he goes, looking at Mum's wine.

'So? What are you saying?'

Dad shrugged. 'Nothing. Maybe I'll join you.'

'Haven't you got a client tonight?'

'She cancelled.'

So he went and poured himself out a big glass of white wine too. I knew what this meant – they'd finish the bottle between them and then they'd be onto another one and quite possibly another one after that, and before the evening was over they'd be into one of their arguments. Not a really bad one. Not a domestic. No physical violence or throwing plates. No need to call the cops. They're not like that. Just a bitter, petty, drunken quarrel about whose turn it was to pay the nursery fees or who forgot to buy more nappies or some shit like that. They'll argue about anything, really. They just don't get on any more, my mum and dad. Well, most of the time they don't. They haven't really got on since Emily was born.

Dad sat down and took a long pull at his white wine. 'Jesus, I've had a hard day.'

Mum was like, 'So have I', as if to say, I bet my day was worse than yours.

I go, 'Yeah, me too.' I bet my day was worse than both of theirs put together.

And I'm not even allowed any wine.

Emily's playing on the carpet now, blowing through the cardboard tube to make farting noises and laughing. She's the only one out of us who hasn't had a hard day. I look at her and I think, Blimey, you just don't know what a rough old world it is out there, do you? I guess that's a good thing. At least we get a few happy years before the crap kicks in.

So, I'm lying in bed that night, thinking about stuff. Renwick's going to kill me. But what do I care, cause if I can't go out with Natalie I might as well be dead anyway. I realised earlier, it came into my head when Mum asked me how my day was, that I've fallen in love. Fallen in love! I don't just fancy Natalie, I don't just want to get her kit off – though I do want to do that, obviously – I'm in love with her. Wow. All my life I've been hearing songs about it and watching films about it and I never really got it until now. Being in love, it's like – it's like nothing else, it's a feeling that takes over your whole body. I just want to moan out loud when I think of Natalie. And it's really miserable, being in love with someone who doesn't love you, it *hurts*. Now I know what people mean when they say their heart aches – but it's a kind of sweet misery, you can get into it, you can even sort of enjoy it.

But how do I know she doesn't love me? What if she does? What if she's just too shy to show it? I've suddenly got this feeling that – well, it's difficult to describe without using really embarrassing language. Like a hot, tender, melting, yearning sort of feeling. I just think, if I was going out with Natalie – and it could happen tomorrow, *tomorrow,* if I just get up the nerve to ask her – and she says yes – if that happens, my life'll be completely different. It'll be like divided in two, the years before Natalie, call them BN, and the years after Natalie, call them AN. And the AN years will be about a million times better – all the crap, like Mum and Dad arguing and snapping at each other all the time, and me worrying about failing all my AS's, and teachers being sarcastic to me, and never having any money, and always getting left out of the football team, and missing buses, and wondering if I look like a jerk in my duffle coat and getting horrible zits and feeling lonely in the evenings – all that crap I just won't *care* about. Because I'll have Natalie. Natalie! Even the name seems sexy, somehow. It makes me think of naughtiness and nakedness and nudity...

It's Valentine's Day on Monday. Maybe she'll send me a Valentine's card. Oh, man, wouldn't that be brilliant. I have to send her one. I'll write a little poem in it. Something about Venus, cause I remember in English Miss Rogers said Venus was the goddess of love. 'Natalie, Natalie, you're my Venus…'

No, that won't work. I can only think of one word to rhyme with Venus and I reckon it would lower the tone a bit.

Never mind, I'll think of something to put on the card. I won't sign it, just maybe put some little clue on it – maybe ask her to meet me somewhere… It could be the best Monday of my life…

But then I think, no, it won't be, cause Steve Renwick's going to kick seven types of shit out of me on Monday after school. I won't be making a date with anyone after that, except the A and E staff at Whipps Cross Hospital. And then I go into a sort of fantasy of me lying in bed in the intensive care unit, all hooked up to tubes and bottles and stuff, with one of those life support machines going bleep-bleep by the side of the bed, and Natalie's come to visit me. I smile at her with bruised, puffy lips and look at her lovingly through my swollen black eyes.

She's like, 'Oh, Adam, you were so brave!'

'Yeah, well, you know… Man's gotta do what a man's gotta do and all that stuff…'

She reaches across and takes my hand. I feel her fingers caressing mine. 'I really admired the way you stood up for yourself. Did you know Steve Renwick's injured too?'

'Is he? What's the matter with him?'

'Bruised knuckles.'

'Oh, right.' There's a bit of a pause. Then I whisper: 'I – I want to tell you something, Natalie.'

'Yes? What is it?'

'I – I love you, Natalie.'

'Oh, Adam – I love you too! I've always loved you!'

'Oh, wow! I'm so happy, Natalie.'

'When you're better, I'll – I'll *show* you how much I love you!'

'Wow.'

'You're – you're all right, aren't you? Down there? In that, you know, region?'

'Bit bruised. But I'll be OK.'

'Could I – could I see?'

It was about this point I must have fallen asleep, and the fantasy continued as a dream.

I won't say any more about that, except just to note that it was a bloody good dream.

When I woke up the next morning, it was with a brilliant idea in my bonce. I knew what to put on Natalie's Valentine's card. And I knew how to ask her out. Two birds with one stone.

Natalie liked playing tennis. So I'd ask her for a game of tennis in the park. After all, why should she say no? I'm crap at tennis, of course. But that didn't matter. In a way it was better, cause then she could teach me. That could create a sort of relationship between us. A bond.

And I'd worked out exactly what words to put on the card:

I

would

Love

to play tennis with

You

That's pretty clever, isn't it? I couldn't see how the plan could fail.

All I needed now was a tennis racket.

'Has anyone got a tennis racket I can borrow?'

Emily was like, 'Wassa tenniswacket?'

It was breakfast time. Emily was sitting with two cushions under her bum to boost her up to table height. She's recently refused to use the high chair any more, because she said it was for babies. She had a bowl of Rice Krispies in front of her, but she kept getting distracted and forgetting to eat them. Sometimes she'd lift the spoon towards her mouth and then stop with it in mid-air while she started jabbering on about something and then all the Rice Krispies would fall off.

It was kind of frustrating to watch. Mum was trying to coax her to eat, in a tone of voice that was so patient it sounded really impatient.

Dad was reading the paper. He and Mum weren't saying anything to each other. Last night's row was still simmering along, obviously.

Dad put his paper down. 'My old racket's somewhere around. Go and have a look in the attic.'

My mum was like, 'I don't want him going up there. It's dangerous.'

Dad goes, 'Dangerous? What are you talking about?'

'He could fall through the rafters.'

'Don't be ridiculous.'

Mum's lips tightened. She turned away and took the spoon from Emily. 'Here you are, Emily, have some of these lovely Krispies, yum yum yum, mmm.'

Emily batted the spoon away and they went flying all over the kitchen.

I was like, 'I'll be careful, Mum, honest.'

'What do you want a tennis racket for, anyway?'

'Cause I'm thinking of having a go at it.'

My dad was like, 'I used to be quite a talented player in my youth, you know.' If you believe him, my dad was talented at just about everything in his youth. 'I played for the county, you know.'

Mum was like, 'Blimey, they must have been desperate.' She says it like it's a joke, but it's the sort of joke that's meant to be annoying. And it works. Now Dad's lips tighten. He picks up his paper.

I was like, 'Well, I'll go up and get it after breakfast. If that's OK.'

'OK,' goes my dad. 'It's one of the old wooden ones. But it's a decent racket. They don't make them like that any more.'

That meant it was crap, obviously. But I didn't mind. It'd give me an excuse for losing to Natalie – plus, it'd be a sort of conversation point. My antique racket, sort of thing. Something to make jokes about. 'That's OK. Any type of racket will do.'

'Wassa wacket?' This is Emily's latest game, asking what everything is.

I'm like, 'It's for playing tennis.'

'Wass tennis?'

'It's a game you play with a ball.'

'Wassa ball?'

'It's a round bouncy thing.'

'Wassa round bouncy fing?'

I go, 'You are!' and pick her up and bounce her on my knee. This makes her laugh and while her mouth's open, Mum spoons in some Rice Krispies. So that's a sort of result.

OK. I'm almost back where we started, now. After breakfast, I got the stepladder out of the garage and lugged it up to the landing. I climbed up and pushed open the trapdoor. I hauled myself up into the darkness and flashed my phone around. Cardboard boxes – an old vacuum cleaner – an old rocking horse – the water tank in the corner – and then, half-hidden under an old rug and a portrait of a sad-looking babe with a harp, my flashlight app picked out the lamp.

Well, you know this bit, right? Eastern-looking lamp, thought of the Antiques Roadshow, picked it up and blew the dust off. Then, to get a better look at it, I got a bit of old sheet and rubbed it.

And that's when things turned seriously weird.

The lamp seemed to sort of twitch in my hands, like it was alive, or like there was something alive inside it. Then a wisp of smoke curled out of the spout, and then the wisp grew into a great big massive column of black smoke. Then the column kind of formed and solidified into the shape of a great big massive enormous genie.

At this point, you must be thinking, *Yeah, right.* And I don't blame you. Cause that's what I thought, too. A genie. Yeah, right. I mean, reality check, or what? I've never believed in crap like that. There's kids at my school who'll swallow anything – like they believe in ghosts and horoscopes and UFOs and conspiracy theories and alien abductions and men in black and the Illuminati and God knows what else, anything as long as it's weird. But I've never been like that. I just believe in stuff you can prove, stuff you can see. But the trouble was, I *could* see this genie. I didn't want to believe it, but I couldn't deny it – he was *there*, hanging in the air in front of me, with his feet a couple of inches off the floor and his turban brushing the ceiling, lit up in the beam of my torch. He was wearing baggy trousers of purple silk and those kind of Turkish shoes that curl up at the ends. His moustache curled up at the ends, too. His chest was bare and brown with an impressive set of pecs. Like, he was built. Ripped. You wouldn't want to get in a fight with him. Steve Renwick wouldn't have stood a chance. No one would. You wouldn't bet on the Incredible Hulk against this guy. Not even with Iron Man and the Mighty Thor backing him up.

So, the genie was like, 'I am the genie of the lamp!'

I was like, 'Right.' Then I go, 'You speak very good English.' This was a moronic thing to say, I know, but I was pretty much in a state of severe shock.

'I speak all languages. You have released me from the lamp. What is your wish?'

'Er – wish? Wodjer mean, wish?'

'Your wish is my command.'

'Oh, right.'

So then I started to think. I knew I had to be careful. In stories, people always blow it. Give them a wish and they waste it. They wish for the first thing that comes into their head, like a sausage sandwich or something. Or they wish for something that sounds good but turns out to have a catch, cause they haven't really thought it through, like they wish to live forever but forget to say anything about not getting old. I didn't want to get caught out. I wanted to get it right.

OK, so this was probably all a hallucination anyway. But suppose, just *suppose* it was real? What would I wish for then? Natalie, obviously. But then, I was still going to get beaten up by Renwick on Monday. I needed a wish to take care of that. It was a pity I didn't have two wishes. And then, there were my AS's and A-levels. It was too bad I didn't have a spare wish so I could get A-stars in all of them without doing any work. Really, I needed *three* wishes.

At least. Cause I'd have liked to wish that my mum and dad would get on better. Hearing them bicker all the time was seriously pissing me off. And I'd have liked to wish I was brilliant at football. And while I was at it, I'd have liked to wish for some money, say a million squid. Or say ten million, why not?

Well, OK, suppose I wished for more wishes? Whenever I read stories about wishes when I was a kid, I always used to wonder why they didn't do this. It seemed so obvious. But would it be allowed?

No harm in trying. Suppose I wished for a million wishes?

'I wish for –'

Then I stopped.

A million wishes seemed plenty. But I knew from the stories that there's always catches in the wishing game. There was this story we did in English with Miss Rogers in Year 8, 'The Monkey's Paw', about this old couple and they've got this magic monkey's paw that gives three wishes. So, the first thing they wish for is two hundred squid, and they get it, but only as compensation, cause their son's got mangled up and killed in the machinery at the factory where he works. So then the woman wishes their son was alive again. And the next thing they hear is this kind of ghastly slithering sound coming up the path, and they realise he's come back to life but he's still all mangled up from the machinery. So then they've got to use the last wish to make him peacefully dead again.

You get the point. The first wish goes wrong and you need another wish to put it right, then that wish goes wrong, so you need another one to put that one right, and so it goes until you run out of wishes. OK, it didn't seem remotely likely that a million wishes would run out before I'd got everything I wanted. But why take a chance? I remembered Tubby in maths going on about infinity. Why not have an infinite number of wishes?

So I was like, 'I wish for an infinite number of wishes.'

The genie looked a bit surprised. He frowned at me. 'Infinite?'

I go, 'Yeah. Is that OK? Can you do it?'

He was like, 'Of course I can do it!' A bit snappy, you know. 'I can grant any wish, provided it's not logically contradictory.'

I wasn't too sure what he meant by this, so I let it go. I was like, 'Well, that's what I want. An infinite number of wishes.'

'Are you sure that is what you want? No one has ever asked for an infinite number of wishes before.'

'Maybe no one's ever really thought it through like me.'

I just didn't see how I could go wrong. Not with an infinite number of wishes.

'Very well,' goes the genie. 'The wishes are yours. To make a wish, simply utter it aloud.'

And then he starts to go fuzzy at the edges. He turns back into a cloud of black smoke. The cloud gets smaller and disappears into the spout of the lamp.

And there I am, standing in the attic on my own, wondering if it was all a dream.

Or maybe I'd gone crazy. Turned into a nutcase. A loony. Barking mad. Completely insane. Let me out of this padded cell or I'll set my genie on you.

Well, there was a simple way to find out.

So I go, 'I wish for a sausage sandwich.'

And the next second, there it was. It just materialised out of thin air. Hot in my hand.

I bit into it. White bread, succulent sausage, with onions and ketchup and mustard in, just how I like it.

Delicious.

So, with my mouth still full, I was like, 'I wish Natalie Forbes was madly in love with me.'

About ten seconds went by, while I stood there in the shadowy attic with my heart beating fast, wondering what was going to happen next.

Then my phone went off. I was so startled I nearly dropped it.

I looked at the caller's name, and it was Natalie.

PART TWO: HOW IT WENT ON FROM THERE

CHAPTER 2

'Hey, Natalie!'

'Hi, Adam. Um…' Her voice is low and breathy and a little hesitant. I feel like I could listen to it all day. 'Hope you don't mind me calling, I just…'

'Don't mind a bit. Good to hear from you.'

'I just – I just felt like speaking to you, Adam. It might sound silly, but… I was sort of…' She giggles. 'I was sort of driven by an impulse.'

'Oh, well, when you're driven by an impulse, you might as well sit back and enjoy the ride, that's what I always say!'

She laughs again. I don't think I've ever made her laugh before. Not like this. Polite laughter, yeah, but not in this low, rich, fruity way, like her whole body thinks it's funny.

'I don't suppose…' said Natalie, '…you wouldn't happen to be free today, would you?'

'I might be able to make myself available.'

'I just feel like I'd like to see you.'

'Would you, Natalie?'

'Yes, I would!'

'Well…' I pretend to be weighing it up. 'I do have kind of a busy day lined up, but maybe I could find a window. Got a meeting with Bill Gates scheduled in but I could probably shift it.'

Natalie laughed again, a pleasant gurgling sound like hot water being poured into Pot Noodles.

'Oh, that would be… I mean I don't want to disrupt your day or anything, but –'

'We could maybe play tennis over at the park?'

'Tennis! I didn't know you played tennis!'

'There's probably a lot of things you don't know about me, Natalie.'

'Ooh, you're a man of mystery, aren't you?'

I was like, 'Yes, I am.' One-second pause. 'Or am I?'

And Natalie laughed for a third time, and the sound was like liquid gold in my ear. Not as in being scalding hot, I mean, but as in being really nice.

'So – how about I meet you over at the park at the tennis courts?'

Natalie was like, 'Sounds like an unimprovable plan!'

One or two things would be an improvement on it, I think. But all in good time.

As I'm setting off for the park, I realise I never did find Dad's racket. But that doesn't matter now. All I have to do is wish for one.

So I do.

And there it is, in my hand. And not a crappy old antique wooden one either, but a brand new spanking high-tension graphite job. A red one. Cool.

There's just one more thing.

'I wish I was good at tennis – just a bit better than Natalie Forbes.'

I could have wished I was the best player in the world, obviously. But that would have been overdoing it. After all, it wouldn't be much of a game if I was belting the ball over the net at a hundred miles an hour like Andy Murray or someone.

The park's full of people. It's a Saturday, and it's sunny, another of those days that feels like a kind of advance instalment on spring. There's a few daffodils and some little purple and white flowers out. And, you know, I start to get a sort of idea about what people mean when they go on about the beauty of nature and all that stuff. To be honest, I used to think people were putting it on a bit, to show off about how sensitive and artistic they were, like that poem we did in English with Miss Rogers in Year 9, about a host of golden daffodils. I mean, I felt like saying to the guy, come on, man, you don't have to make such a song and dance about it. It's only daffodils for Christ's sake. Get a grip. But now I'm getting a sort of glimmering of what he was on about. The daffodils do look great. And so do the little purple and white flowers. And so do the trees, even though they haven't got their leaves yet. And so does the blue sky, and so do the little white clouds gently sailing across it. And so does Natalie – oh, my God, so does Natalie. The minute I see her I forget all about the beauty of nature. The beauty of Natalie, that's all I'm interested in.

She's standing next to the tennis courts, and she's wearing a pair of little white shorts. Hey, that rhymes. I didn't mean to do that. She's got on a white T-shirt with a picture of Albert Einstein sticking his tongue out on it, and she's tapping her tennis racket against her trainers. Wow. I mean, what a picture. I can't help staring at her legs. I've never looked at them properly before, and anyway she normally wears tights. They're kind of longer than I thought, but not too skinny, very shapely, in fact, with rounded calves, very pale, and very smooth. Does she shave them, I wonder? Or are they naturally smooth? It's still a bit early in the year to have bare legs and I notice she's got little tiny goose pimples, and I don't know why, but that seems really, like, exciting.

Natalie's like, 'Isn't it a lovely day?'

'Too right!'

'There's no one on the courts – shall we get started?'

'Yeah, let's do it!' And then I go, 'Play tennis, I mean!' – in case she thinks I'm making a, you know, indecent proposal, and then I realise that she'd never have thought that if I hadn't drawn attention to it. But then she laughs, and I realise it's OK. I don't have to worry about saying the wrong thing any more and feeling embarrassed. Natalie loves me now. She's not going to find fault with what I say. She's on my side.

'Tennis first,' she goes. 'And then – well, we'll see!'

And she gives a little wicked smile – totally different to her normal expression, which is usually kind of serious. And I'm like, 'Wow!'

So, anyway, we start this game of tennis. And I start to get what people see in this game – when you can play a bit, when you get a rally going and the ball goes 'Pock! Pock! Pock! Pock!' zipping low over the net, and you're making these elegant strokes, you know – well, it's still not as good as football, but there's definitely something in it.

'Hey, you're good!' goes Natalie, after I've won the first game.

I'm like, 'Yeah, well, I don't get to play that much, you know, but I reckon I haven't got a bad eye for the ball.'

Natalie corrects me. 'A superb eye for the ball!'

'Well, I wouldn't go that far, you know…'

Halfway through the match, when I'm winning 4–2, the park-keeper comes bustling onto the court. He's a short but stocky kind of guy, with broad shoulders, a red face, an incredibly bad temper and tattooed arms – not those cool, decorative, abstract Maori-style tats, but bulldogs and eagles and daggers and skulls with snakes writhing out of their eye-sockets. I used to be dead frightened of him when I was a kid, and I still am a bit. I sometimes think he's the kind of guy who'd just go mad one day and murder a load of people with that pointed stick he uses for picking up the rubbish, and it would be all in the papers – 'Neighbours commented that he always kept himself to himself' and all that stuff.

'Did you book this court?' Well, of course he knows perfectly well we didn't book it, cause he's the guy who takes the bookings.

I'm like, 'Well, there was no one on it, you know, so we thought…'

'So you thought you'd get away without paying!'

In the past, at this point I'd have got all nervous and apologetic and started saying, 'No, no, honestly' and stuff. But now I've got my wishes, I don't need to be nervous of anything. So, I'm like, 'How much?'

'It's eight pounds sixty, plus a pound for the booking fee!'

'What booking fee? We just turned up and it was empty.'

'Don't argue the toss with me, sonny!'

For a minute, I wonder whether to get angry about this. I could teach the guy a lesson he wouldn't forget if I felt like it. I could wish that all the squirrels in the park would go mad and attack him, jumping on him and gnawing his nose off, or something. But then I think… Nah, it's a lovely day, Natalie loves me, let's not spoil it with any unpleasantness. Under my breath, I mutter 'I wish I had a hundred quid' and I feel a sort of little nudge as it materialises inside my tracksuit pocket.

'Here,' I go, shoving the money at him. 'All right?'

'What's this? I only asked for nine pounds sixty!'

'That's all right, mate. Keep the change.'

His little eyes dart from me to the money and from the money to me. 'Is this a wind-up?'

'Here, just take it. And don't bother us again.'

He reaches out cautiously and takes the money as though it's going to chomp his hand off if he's not careful. 'Well – all I can say is – thank you very much indeed – it's very generous of you, sir…'

He's gone all respectful now – so respectful that he walks off the court backwards, bumping into the gate on his way out.

Natalie's come up to the net. 'Wow – that put him in his place! How much did you give him?'

'Dunno. Didn't count it.'

Natalie giggles. 'Wow! You're so cool, Adam!'

'Oh, you know – that's just the kind of guy I am…'

After we'd finished the set – which I won 6–3, just thought I'd mention that – we went for a walk through the park. I bought ice creams and we strolled past the duck pond, licking them. The ice creams, I mean, not the ducks. I liked the way the ice cream made a little moustache on Natalie's upper lip. It made me want to lick it off. And then I thought, well, why not?

So I'm like, 'Hold still a minute' – and then I take her by the arms and I lick the ice cream off her lip – and the next minute, we're snogging like we're representing Great Britain in the Olympic Freestyle Snogging Event, right there in the middle of the path.

I can feel her tongue frisking around inside my mouth, and my tongue frisking against hers, it's like two seals playing together, and her soft warm body is pressed up against me, and it's just like – it's almost too much for me to take, if you want to know the truth. It's so fantastic that I almost want to stop, and go off somewhere on my own for a bit, so I can think about her properly. Only I don't really want to leave her. It's like I want to be with her and on my own at the same time.

After a while we step apart a little and look at each other. I'm breathing hard. And then Natalie fixes her clear, green bespectacled eyes on mine, and says in a low, serious voice, 'I love you, Adam.'

For a minute, I don't say a word. To tell the truth, I'm a bit overcome with emotion. Cause no one – except my parents, I guess, when I was a really little kid – has ever said they loved me before. And even though I know she's only saying it cause of my wish, it kind of gets to me.

Natalie's like, 'I know this must be a shock. To be honest it was a shock to me. It swept over me this morning like a – like a great big tsunami – how much I love you. I hope you don't mind.'

'No, I don't mind at all, it's, er… It's really nice.' This is about as ridiculous an understatement as saying that the stars are a long way off, or that atoms are on the small side.

'I know it's too much to expect that you'd feel the same.'

'Not at all. I, er, do.'

'You –?' She stares at me, eyes suddenly bright, mouth half-open, as if she's witnessing a breathtaking sunrise or something. And I become conscious somehow that my face is mimicking hers, as if I'm seeing the sunrise too. 'What do you mean, you mean you…?'

'Yeah, I mean, I…' I'm finding it hard to get the words out. I'm all choked up with emotion.

'What? Say it, Adam, don't play games with me!'

'I love you,' I whisper.

Natalie falls into my arms again, and buries her head in my shoulder. She mumbles something.

'What was that?'

Natalie raises her head a little and in a quiet, clear voice, she's like, 'I want to *show* you how much I love you.'

I just stare at her, not saying anything for a bit. She's used the exact same words as in my fantasy. For a minute, I wonder if I'm sitting in that Experience Machine Dirk was going on about, imagining it all. Cause this has got to be too good to be true.

Hasn't it?

'My parents are out this afternoon. We could go back to my place – what do you say?'

There's only one word I can say to this. And it's 'Wow!'

Natalie's house is dead quiet. You can tell it's empty as soon as you go in the door. Like, it doesn't just sound quiet, it feels quiet.

'Shall we go up to my bedroom?'

I'm like, 'Er, yes please.' Then I think that sounded a bit wimpish, so I go, 'That'd be cool.' My voice has gone all hoarse and croaky.

The carpet's soft and deep and our feet make almost no noise as we go up the stairs. Natalie goes first and I can see her beautiful round bum in her tight white tennis shorts, going up the stairs in front of me. I feel like I'm in a dream. My heart's beating like a machine gun.

'Here we are.' She pushes open a door.

I look round her bedroom. It's kind of impressive. Like, my room's just a tip, with clothes and trainers and stuff all over the floor. And there's nothing really interesting in it. Well, there's my PlayStation 4 and a few games scattered about the place. There's a bookcase with a few books about football, and my collection of comics and graphic novels – I used to get them for free from Dad's shop. But that's about it. But Natalie's room is like, I don't know, an art gallery or something. There's a poster on the wall above the bed of some little kid holding a dove, and another one opposite of three guys in blue robes standing by the sea shore, and another one of a sort of rickety yellow chair with a pipe on it. And on the dressing table there's lots of nice little ornaments, like a dragon made out of sea-shells and a white china unicorn. And there's a shelf full of books with black spines – Penguin Classics. I look a bit closer and see there's a Jane Austen there, and Emily Bronte, and I think, blimey, she actually reads that stuff, and it's not even on the A-level syllabus.

But I don't waste any more time looking at the books. There's Natalie to look at. She's standing in the middle of the room, smiling at me. She opens her arms out wide.

'How about another kiss?'

'Yeah, that'd be cool,' I go in my croaky voice.

So we kiss, and it's cool. And then she goes, 'It's hot in here, isn't it?'

'Well, yeah, it's on the warm side...'

'What do you think we should do?'

'Er, I dunno, maybe turn the central heating down...'

'We could do that... or...' She gives the naughtiest smile you could possibly imagine. 'We take some of our clothes off?'

'Yeah, that'd be… cool.' I can hardly get the words out.

So Natalie starts to strip off. And in a couple of moments she's standing there just in a white bra and knickers. And me, I'm down to my pants. It's a good job I'm wearing my best ones today. My blue Calvin Kleins.

'Maybe we'd better take the rest off – what do you think?'

'Yeah, that'd be cool,' I manage to croak. Any second now, and I'm going to see Natalie Forbes in the nude.

Natalie in the nude!

I've spent hours fantasising about this moment. And now it's going to happen for real!

For real. Yeah, well sort of. But there's just one thing bothering me.

The way Natalie is now, all like sexy and loving, with her eyes all lit up and that little wicked smile – it's all totally fantastic, there's no doubt about that, but I just kind of wish it was more – I wish it was more to do with *me*, you know? She wasn't like this before the wish. And now she is. So it's obvious that it's only the wish that's making her be like this. And the thing is, I want to be loved for… well, for being *me*, you know? Not cause the genie's making her love me. I want her to choose me of her own free will. But there's nothing I can do about that now, is there?

But there is, of course. I can do anything, now, with my infinite number of wishes. What I want is for Natalie's normal self to love me. So – just as she's unhooking the clasp at the back of her bra – I go, 'I wish you were your normal self again, Natalie.'

And as soon as I've said it, I think, *Oh Christ on the crapper, what have I done?* The smile freezes on Natalie's lips. She stops unhooking the clasp at the back of her bra. Another second, and it would have been on the floor at her feet. But the bra stays on. A new expression comes over her face – kind of bewildered and alarmed.

'Look, I – I think we must have got a bit carried away here…'

'OK, let's get carried away a bit further!'

But I know it's hopeless. My voice isn't hoarse and croaking any more. There's nothing to be nervous about now. It's over. I've blown it. And all my desire just drains away. I feel like I've had a bucket of cold water thrown over me.

'No, I'm sorry – I don't know what came over me.' She snatches up her clothes and holds them in front of her like a screen. 'I'm sorry, but could you go now?'

'Don't I even get a cup of tea?'

'No, I don't think that's a good idea. I want to be on my own.'

'Oh, right.'

Obviously, she can hear the disappointment in my voice, cause she starts to look sad and a little bit guilty. 'Look, I'm sorry,' she goes. 'I know it must look as if I've led you up the garden path. But – look, I can't explain it, something came over me, it was – as if I was taken over. I feel really bad about it. But – can we just forget about it? Pretend it never happened?'

'Yeah, sure.'

'We can still be friends, can't we?'

'Yeah, whatever,' I mumble. Then I turn round, go out the room, down the stairs, out the front door and into the street, and I'm hoping all the time that she'll call me back. But she doesn't, of course.

I bet I know what you're thinking. Why didn't I just wish that she was in love with me again, and carry on where we left off? Well, I did think of that, right, but something stopped me. It would have seemed a bit, I don't know, kind of tacky, now that I'd seen what her real feelings were. I mean, what I really wanted was for her to be in love with me without me having to wish it. But obviously, that was the one thing I couldn't wish for. I started to get an inkling of what the genie meant when he said he couldn't grant wishes that were logically contradictory.

What was really bothering me was, I'd seen how Natalie acted when she was in love, and I'd seen how she acted towards me when she was her normal self, and there was a big difference. And one day, when she fell in love for real, some lucky guy was going to get all that, the eyes lit up and the wicked little smile and stuff, and that lucky guy wouldn't be me.

I started to feel jealous of the guy, without even knowing who he was.

Anyway. I got home. No one was in. Dad was out instructing. I knew that because he'd been going on about it earlier. He had Mrs Sprocket this afternoon, the woman who was so anxious she drove with her foot on the brake all the time. Mum and Emily must have gone shopping.

I realised I was still holding the tennis racket. I looked at it in a frustrated kind of way and then I was like, 'I wish you were a bunch of flowers.' It turned into a great big colourful bouquet immediately, and I shoved it in a vase and stuck it on the dining-room table. It'd be a nice surprise for Mum.

I felt like talking to someone, so I called Dirk, but he didn't pick up. I thought about sending him a text, but what could I say in it? *Hey guess wot i have infinite wishes CUL8R.* It didn't seem right. A text didn't seem... *weighty* enough for news like that.

So I sat at the foot of the stairs in the hall and put my chin in my hands, in what you might call a pensive pose. It was the first time I'd had a chance to stop and think about the position I was in, with all these wishes. I mean, what was I going to do with them? Was there anything at all I could do about Natalie? I wanted her to love me but I wanted it to be of her own accord. But I couldn't *wish* she'd love me of her own accord, cause then it wouldn't be of her own accord...

Bobbligrubs came snuffling up and stuck his head on my knee. And I thought, what a good dog. I reached out and stroked his head. You can trust dogs. They don't let you down. Not like girls. No wonder they call them man's best friend.

I was like, 'Come on, Bobbligrubs. Let's go for a walk.'

At the sound of this magic word, Bobbligrubs started capering round and chasing his tail and jumping up and down like a mad thing. Bobbligrubs is a great dog. He's black and skinny with a wiry coat, long legs and a square, intelligent face. A man in a pub garden when we were on holiday in Devon once called him a 'classic mongrel', and that's about right.

So, we set off round the block, and Bobbligrubs frisked about, sniffing things, 100% glad to be alive, and I almost felt a kind of envy. I mean, it was so easy to make him happy. I wished he could talk and tell me how it felt. I'd had this wish a thousand times, ever since I was a really little kid. But now, I suddenly realised, I could make it come true. So I was like, out loud, 'I wish you could talk, Bobbligrubs.'

Bobbligrubs raised his head from the tree he'd been sniffing at and turned and looked at me, and his mouth opened, and then he was like, in this gruff, snuffly voice, 'Aw, smell that. Get a load of that. Aw, that's lovely. That's that little Scottie down the road. Aw, she's a sexy little beast, she is. I'd give her one any day, I would. Aw yes, give her a portion all right, I certainly would give her a portion, know what I mean?' Then he sniffed at the tree trunk again. 'Aw, yes, aw, yes, get a load of that, what a sexy smell, I know who that is, that's the Labrador opposite, saucy little bitch she is, saucy big bitch, I mean, but I like a bit of meat on a bitch, I'd give her a portion any day of the week, and that's official. Aw, who's this? It's that pit bull from number 37, thinks he's well hard, he does. He's not so hard, he'd better not try anything with me, that's all. I could take him out any day of the week, I'd chew the bastard's legs off, I would...'

'OK, OK,' I go, kind of hastily. 'I wish you couldn't talk any more.'

Bobbligrubs fell silent. He carried on snuffling round the tree as if nothing had happened.

I felt as if there was a lesson in there somewhere, but I couldn't work out what it was.

When we got back, Dad was home.

'Hi. How was Mrs Sprocket?'

Dad shuddered and closed his eyes. 'Don't. A nightmare.' He went to the fridge and got himself a beer. 'Enough to drive anyone to drink, this job.'

'Can I have one?'

'No.' He sat down and took a long pull at his beer. 'I suppose I should count myself lucky I still have people to teach. In a few years when these driverless cars come in, what am I going to do then?'

'I don't know, what are you going to do then?'

'I don't know, do I, that's why I said what am I going to do then?'

The front door opened and Mum came in laden down with Tesco bags and Emily.

'Hello, Em!'

''Ello, Adam!'

I picked her up and swung her round, making her scream.

Mum's like, 'Mind her head!' Then she saw the flowers on the dining room table. 'Where did these come from?'

'From me, Mum. I got them for you.'

Mum's face breaks into a smile. 'How sweet of you, Adam!' Then the smile fades away. 'I might have known they wouldn't be from you,' she goes to my dad. 'When did you last get me flowers?'

Dad shrugs. 'When did you last get me any?'

'Don't be ridiculous, that's not the point.'

'I'm not being ridiculous. And it is the point.'

'The man is supposed to buy the flowers for the woman. As well you know.'

'I thought we lived in an age of gender equality.'

Mum laughs a bitter laugh. 'Yeah, right – a lot you know about gender equality.'

I can see Dad shaping up for some angry answer and I decide I've had enough of this. I mean, I'm just about sick of it. So I go, 'I wish you two would just kiss and make up.'

The funny thing is, I hadn't even meant to make a wish, I was just saying how I felt. But as soon as I'd said it, Mum and Dad stopped arguing. Dad got up and gave Mum a great big hug and they gave each other a great big smacking kiss. I couldn't remember the last time I'd seen them do this. Emily laughed and clapped her hands at the unfamiliar sight.

Unfortunately, it didn't last. I was upstairs in my room a bit later, eating another sausage sandwich I'd just wished for, when I heard them having a go at each other again. Arguing about sweetcorn, this time. Mum had got tinned instead of frozen and Dad didn't like it. They'd had a few drinks by that time, of course.

I muttered a wish that they'd calm down and make it up again. Everything went quiet, and then I heard them chatting away quite amicably. So that was all right. At least for the time being. But what was the deal here? I tried to work out the logic of it. I'd wished they'd make it up and they did. So the wish had worked. But I hadn't wished they'd *stay* made up. The, like, structural tensions in their relationship – and the booze – had made it all go tits-up again. If I wanted a solution that would last on its own I'd need to make more specific wishes. So that they were each getting what they wanted out of the relationship. And that sounded like a tricky and possibly embarrassing business.

Besides – did I have the *right* to interfere with people's emotions at, you know, a deep level? I'd tried it once with Natalie and that hadn't totally gone according to plan. And I wondered, if I hadn't wished she didn't love me any more, whether in time she'd simply have gone off me of her own accord anyway. And then I'd have had to keep topping up the wish, repeatedly wishing she loved me, like pouring water into a leaky bottle.

This was going to be hard to handle. I felt like someone who's just jumped on a jet-powered skateboard and then realised he doesn't have the first idea how to skate. Better lay off making wishes about people's emotions, I decided. At least till I knew what I was doing a bit better.

I yawned.

It had been quite a day.

CHAPTER 3

'Whoa! Nice jacket!'

'Thanks.'

I'd called for Dirk on the way to school as usual. It was Monday morning. But for me it wasn't the usual sort of Monday morning, not the Oh-shit-it's-Monday-a-whole-week-of-school-to-come-I-wish-I'd-stayed-in-bed sort of Monday morning. Today I was looking forward to it. The fight with Renwick was on, and I was going to make history. I was feeling light-hearted and kind of light-headed. The sunny weather was continuing. But that wasn't surprising. I'd wished for it. Along with my new jacket.

Dirk was like, 'That is one cool jacket,' as we walked up the road together. 'Where'd you get it?'

'Oh, I got it, er, online. Stone Island website, you know.'

Dirk's jaw dropped. 'It's a Stone Island jacket?'

'Sure. Take a look at the label if you don't believe me.'

It truly was a beautiful piece of work, that jacket. It was padded, and it was white ('ice white', it said on the website) with black buttons and a black fur collar. And it made my shitty old duffle coat look like, well, a shitty old duffle coat. I was also wearing a new pair of black Adidas trainers I'd wished for (Adidas stands for All Day I Dream About Sex, but I expect you knew that). I liked the combination of my white jacket and black trainers. It was cool. I had to keep turning my head when I walked past shop windows to admire myself.

'But – how did you afford it, man? They cost about a grand, those Stone Island coats!'

'Eleven hundred, mate.'

'Where the hell did you get eleven hundred from?'

'Oh, you know – saving up a bit here and there – I had some money left over from my birthday...'

You see, I hadn't told Dirk about the wishes yet. I hadn't told anyone. I wasn't sure I was going to. I wasn't too sure how people would take it.

'I hope Renwick doesn't make too much of a mess of it.'

'That's OK. There's nothing to worry about there.'

'You're really going ahead with it?'

'Sure I am. Why not?'

'Some people might say not getting your head kicked in's a pretty good reason.'

'Some people are gonna get a surprise.'

'You could still back out, you know. Just tell Renwick you've had second thoughts. You'll get called a chicken, but at least you won't get your neck broke.'

'Just chill your beans, man. I'll be OK.'

Dirk shook his head. 'I dunno if you're a hero or a nut-job. But if you're really going through with it…'

'Course I'm going through with it.'

'Well, I've been thinking about this, and I've got a bit of advice.'

'Yeah?'

'Here's what to do. Just before the fight's supposed to start, smash him in the face. Like, before he's ready, just when he's taking his jacket off. Hard as you can. Then, whatever happens after that, you'll have got one good hit in.'

I'd had a long hard think over the weekend about the best way to deal with Renwick. I could have just wished to beat the crap out of him and left it at that. But that would have seemed a bit, I don't know, kind of… *inartistic*. I wanted to do something special. I thought of wishing I was as strong as a gorilla. But that might have been a bit dangerous. I mean, I might have pulled his head off by accident or something. I didn't want to actually kill the guy. That would be a bit… severe. Then I had what seemed a pretty good idea at first – I'd wish that every time Renwick hit me, he'd feel the force of it twice as much as me. Like, he'd bash me on the nose and his own nose would break. So every time he hit me he'd be getting knocked over, but he wouldn't be able to see where the punches were coming from. It would have been kind of funny, but I dropped that idea in the end. Cause it still involved me getting punched, and that was something I wanted to avoid. In the end, though, I got it. It took a lot of thinking, but I landed on the perfect idea. Renwick wouldn't know what had hit him.

'See what I mean?' goes Dirk. 'You might as well get one good hit in.'

'Oh, I'll get a lot more than one good hit in. Just you wait and see.'

The first person we saw when we went in the school gates was —
    have a guess...
    that's right.
    Steve Renwick.

He was leaning against the wall with three or four of his followers – he's got these stupid followers who follow him around; they think he's the dog's bollocks cause he's so hard. They're not hard themselves, they're just trying to pick up a bit of reflected glory. Anyway, the followers all looked at me and grinned. One of them – Mervyn Stott his name is, stupid name, if you ask me – started chanting quietly, 'You're going home in a bleeding ambulance'. That's a stupid chant, I've always thought. Doesn't even make sense. If you were in an ambulance you wouldn't be going home, would you? You'd be going to hospital.

'Shame to get blood all over that nice new coat!' said another follower. His name was Ethan Crump.

The grins intensified. Except in the case of Renwick. He didn't grin. He just fixed his icy blue eyes on a point a thousand yards behind my head, and he was like, 'Phoned that undertaker, then?'

'Yeah, I did. I asked him to come round and pick you up from the waste ground, about five past four.'

Renwick widened his eyes so he looked even more of a psycho. He stopped leaning against the wall and stood up straight. He pointed his finger at me, with his thumb cocked up behind, like it was a gun.

'Don't try and be funny, sonny,' he goes in this kind of quiet, menacing voice. 'You'll make it worse for yourself if you do.'

I'm like, 'Oh no, I'm quaking with fear.'

Renwick's voice gets even quieter and even more menacing. 'Right. I was gonna let you off lightly, Gowers. Just slap you around a bit. But not any more. You're dead.'

I'm like, 'Is that right, Renwick? Is that right?' Then I turn and stroll into school, with Dirk.

Dirk's like, 'Death wish, man. A death wish, that's what it is.'

I just smiled.

What with this showdown with Renwick, I hadn't been thinking much about Natalie. I mean, I had been thinking about her, but not with the front part of my mind. When I saw her standing outside Tubby's room, waiting to go in for double economics, I felt this kind of jolt, like a little electric shock. But I didn't show it. I was like, 'Hi, Natalie.' Casual, you know.

Natalie was like, 'hi,' in a small voice, looking down at the floor. Still embarrassed about Saturday, obviously. And I had been wondering about wishing she'd forget it, so I could start all over again. But then I thought, why should she forget she was once in love with me? Is it such an unbearable thing to remember? It's kind of insulting to me, isn't it?

'Hi, Adam,' goes Claire. 'Hey, nice jacket!'

'Thanks.'

'You're a real Beau Brummie!'

'That's Brummel,' corrected Natalie. Claire's got this habit of getting expressions slightly wrong.

'Where'd you get it?' That was Shushmita.

'What, this old thing? Picked it up in a charity shop.'

Claire's like, 'You never!' She's laughing, and so is Shushmita. Natalie isn't, unfortunately. It's like she's made a solemn vow never to laugh at any of my jokes. Still, she is looking at me. At least that suggests a certain amount of interest. Before we can say anything else, Tubby comes sweeping along. And I mean sweeping, cause he always wears one of those old-fashioned black gowns that you only see in comics. He's even got one of those stupid flat hats with a tassel on, but he only wears it at the end of term. Thinks he's a bit of a character, Tubby.

'Good morning, all – are we ready once again to drink at the well of knowledge?'

No one bothered to answer this, of course. Tubby unlocked the room and in we went. I sat in my usual place by the window and just stared out of it, deliberately paying no attention to the lesson. I knew it wouldn't be long before Tubby picked on me, and I couldn't wait. Yesterday, you see, I'd wished I was brilliant at economics, and statistics and probability and everything connected with it. It was well weird when I picked up the textbook to check. All those pages and pages of charts and graphs and numbers and symbols – in the past it might as well have been Chinese as far as I was concerned, but now I could just read it straight off, like it was a comic or something. I couldn't understand why I'd ever thought it was difficult.

'Adam,' goes Tubby after a while, 'is anything interesting happening outside that window? Any real-life dramas that the rest of us should be aware of?'

'Not really.'

'Not really, I see. Perhaps you were thinking of "nothing" again?'

A few lame-brains laughed at this.

'Can't remember.'

'You can't remember, I see. Well, let's see how much you remember about probability, shall we? Do you remember the hat?'

'Yeah.'

'What was in it?'

'Raffle tickets.'

'Raffle tickets, that's right. Only now, there are not two different colours, but three. We have ten red, seven green and fifteen blue. Do you follow?'

'Yeah.'

'So, Adam, perhaps you could tell us all how to work out the probability, if you took three tickets without looking, that you'd have one of each colour?'

'Course I could.'

'Well then, perhaps you would,' goes Tubby, with this kind of tired patience that gets another laugh.

Most people, even if they knew how to do the sum, would have had to get their calculator out at this point. But not me. I'm like '1 in 28.342857146,' quick as a flash.

There's a bit of a silence. Tubby stares at me.

'Or if you want it expressed as a decimal,' I go, 'it's .03528225806.'

Tubby checks this on his calculator. Then he looks at me in amazement. I can see he suspects a trick, but he can't work out what it could be.

'Er – yes – correct. And, could you tell me, how did you arrive at that answer?'

'It's very simple, Mr Tubby,' I go, all innocent like. 'The probability that the first one you take out is blue is 15 in 32. The probability that the next one is red is 10 in 31. The probability that the last one is green is 7 in 30. Multiply 15 by 10 by 7, then multiply 32 by 31 by 30, divide the first figure by the second, and you've got the answer. It doesn't make any difference what order they come out in, of course.'

'No – er – of course,' goes Tubby. 'And, you did all the calculations in your head?'

'Oh yes. Well, it's quicker than a calculator, innit?'

My triumph is complete. Dirk's staring at me. Everyone's staring at me. I throw a quick glance over my shoulder to see if Natalie's staring at me, and she is. When she sees me looking round, she looks down at her desk. But she must have been impressed, mustn't she? I mean, she must have been, mustn't she?

I mean, she must.

Mustn't she?

'Hey, nice boots!'

'Yeah, they're not bad, are they?'

I was lacing up my brand new Nike Hypervenom Phantom 3 football boots. Very fine-looking, streamlined shoes, matt black with wicked blue studs and the Nike swoosh in white on the heel like the wings of Mercury, messenger of the gods. Sorry, got a bit poetic there.

Martin's like, 'They must have set you back a bit.'

'The best doesn't come cheap, Martin. The best doesn't come cheap.'

Martin grinned. 'Let's hope they make you play better!'

'You know what, I reckon they might.'

We left the changing-rooms and ran out onto the school field. It was a double free period and Mr Nossiter had agreed to ref the game. About another fifteen kids had shown up. The February sun wasn't warm but it was super-bright and made the grass glow a gorgeous radioactive green. I felt the cold air in my lungs and a restless energy in my limbs. This was going to be fun. I'd wished I was the best at football in the school.

Mr Nossiter was like, 'All right, we got turned over 4–1 by Norlington Road at the weekend, so I'm looking for a distinct improvement from everybody. Martin, Desmond, you be captains and pick sides.'

Martin Bone and Desmond Jesmond were the two best players – I mean they had been before I made my wish – and thought they still were. Martin picked me first, which was pretty decent of him, considering he must have thought I was still my usual crap self at football. Sometimes friendship comes before tactics.

'Thanks, Martin.'

''Sall right. Had to have you in my team with those boots, didn't I?'

Nossiter blew his whistle.

And I was on it like a winged god.

I swooped in and dispossessed Desmond Jesmond, whipping the ball off his toe so neatly he didn't even realise what had happened at first, but carried on running for a few steps as if he still had the ball. I scorched down the wing, effortlessly dodging or jumping over tackles.

Martin was calling for it in the box. I whipped in a perfect, curling cross that he met with his head. The ball shot downwards, past the goalie's outstretched arm, and buried itself in the bottom corner of the net. It was beautiful, like a diagram in a physics textbook showing how the angle of incidence equals the angle of deflection.

I ran to Martin and we high-fived each other.

Martin was grinning all over his face. 'Looks like those boots work, Adam!'

That kind of set the pattern for the rest of the game. Me and Martin bossed the show. Martin got another goal, and I scored a hat-trick. But it wasn't just the goals – I was everywhere, making runs, tracking back, tackling, passing. I was so good I was able to make the other players on my side good too, if that makes sense.

Nossiter came up to me when the game was over. 'That was quite a display, Adam.'

'Thanks.'

'Would you be free to turn out for the school team on Sunday?'

The waste ground behind the school used to be a field, in fact the school used to use it for sports, but that was years ago and it's all neglected and gone to seed now. It's full of rubbish, not just tin cans and fag-ends and stuff but old tyres and supermarket trolleys, even an old telly. It doesn't belong to the school any more, they sold it to a developer to build flats but then the developer went bust. There's a massive steel fence around it, but there's lots of places you can get in. In a funny kind of way though, the school still does use it for sports, cause whenever there's a big fight, this is where it happens. This is the place where Steve Renwick beat up Matt Hardy when he was only in Year 8 and Matt Hardy was Year 10. This is the place where Desmond Jesmond had his epic battle with Hassan Arif, and where he beat up Nick Carker so badly he was off school for three days. And this is the place where Renwick took on both the Johnson twins at once and beat the crap out of them.

I was at all those fights – it's not that I particularly like watching fights, right, but if there's a rumble going on and everyone's talking about it, well, it's just human nature to go and watch it, isn't it? I remember how sorry I felt for the kids who got beaten up. You could see the fear in their eyes before the fight, they knew they were going to get their heads kicked in but they had to go through with it. If it hadn't been for my wishes, I'd have been in the exact same position now. I'd have been shitting bricks. As it is, I'm standing there with my hands in my pockets, cool as a cucumber.

'How you feeling?' goes Dirk.

'Cool. Don't you worry.'

Martin was like, 'You don't have to go through with it, you know. Don't want you to get injured before the game on Sunday!'

'Injuries might well occur. But not to me!'

Dirk looked at me kind of curiously. 'You're really not scared at all, are you?'

'Nah. Renwick won't know what's hit him.'

Here he was now, coming through a gap in the fence with his stupid followers tagging along behind like ducklings following their mum. They all pretended to be surprised to see me there.

'Well, at least he turned up!' goes Mervyn Stott and they all laugh. There's a few other kids arriving through other gaps in the fence, spectators – you know. They're in high spirits, laughing and talking loudly, excited but a bit nervous too, I reckon. They know they're going to see some blood.

And they're right.

'You ready?' goes Renwick.

'Yeah.'

And the next moment he's coming at me, so fast, I've hardly got time to get my wish out. But I just manage to mutter it before he reaches me, 'I wish I could move ten times as fast as normal', and then Renwick slows right down. Or that's how it looks from my perspective, anyway. It looks like Renwick is moving underwater – no, slower than that, like he's moving through porridge or custard. Think how fast I can move now – ten times as fast as normal. That means I could run the hundred metres in under a second and a half. In comparison, everyone around me seems to be moving like they're in a slo-mo replay on *Match of the Day*. Slower than that, in fact. It's weird. Mervyn Stott and the others are shouting – I can see their mouths moving, but I can't hear what they're shouting – probably, 'Kill him, Renwick!' and shit like that, but to my super-fast ears it just sounds like a long, low, very deep rumbling. Well weird.

I wait for Renwick to aim the first blow. Here it comes, his arm swinging slowly through the air towards me. Behind his fist I can see Renwick's face, the psychotic blue eyes, the teeth gritted, the whole face screwed up in slo-mo anger. When his fist is about an inch from my face I step aside and whack him on the side of the head.

It hurts my hand quite badly, like I've hit a tree or something. But not as bad as it hurts him. Gradually, he starts to turn towards me. On his face is a slow dawning outrage and bewilderment. I can see his foot starting to come up now – it looks like he's trying to kick me in the balls. Yeah, right. Like that's gonna happen.

I move behind him, take careful aim, and kick him up the arse as hard as I can. He's off balance, with one foot off the ground, so he has to fall. But he falls so slowly, I've easily got time to move round to the other side and whack him on the other side of his head, not quite as hard as before – I don't want to break my hand – and then I still have time to move round to the front again and, with a left-right combination, punch him on the chin and the nose, and he's not even halfway to the ground yet.

I could go on, but you've to know when to stop. I didn't want to make *too* much of a mess of him. I was like, 'I wish I was back to normal speed now.'

Crash! Renwick hits the ground. The world picks up its usual speed again. Renwick's followers look almost as stunned as he does. The low rumbling from the crowd becomes an excited babble.

'Did you see that?'

'How many times did he hit him?'

'Dunno, man – he was like a blur!'

'Never seen anything like it!'

Martin was like, 'How the hell did you *do* that?'

'It's all about timing, Mart.'

I reach out to Dirk for my Stone Island jacket. He gives it to me without saying a word. I'm like, 'Let's go.'

As we're leaving through a gap in the fence, I look back and see Renwick has managed to sit up. His nose is bleeding, and he's shaking his head like he's trying to clear something loose that's rattling around inside it.

'OK, man,' goes Dirk. We're halfway home and these are the first words he's uttered. 'Come on, tell me. What's going on, for Christ's sake?'

'Wodjer mean?'

'Come on, Adam – that wasn't normal, what happened back there.'

'I dunno what you mean. I had a fight, I won. End of.'

'No, but – how did you move like that? It's – like, I've never seen anyone move so fast! I mean, you beat the crap out of him in about two seconds!'

I shrugged. 'No point dragging it out.'

'And that's not all,' Dirk goes. 'Cause how come you're suddenly brilliant in Economics – solving probability problems without a calculator? And I heard about your exploits at football in the afternoon. And how come you're wearing a Stone Island jacket to school? There's something weird going on here.'

And suddenly I just think, why not? He looks so puzzled and desperate for information, it wouldn't be fair to keep him in the dark. Plus, I'm starting to feel the need to confide in someone. All this weirdness – it's hard to take on your own.

'Well, the fact is, Dirk,' I go, 'I've got an infinite number of wishes.'

'What?'

'It's true. A genie gave them to me.'

'What?'

'I met him in the attic.'

'What?'

'I wish you'd stop saying "what".'

Dirk tries to say it again, but can't, obviously. His lips are like pursed together in the shape of a letter O, but he can't make a sound. After a bit he gives up and tries another tack. 'Let me get this straight,' he goes. 'You just make a wish and it comes true?'

'You got it.'

'And you can wish for anything?'

'Anything that's not logically contradictory. That's what the genie said.'

'And there's no limit on the number of wishes?'

'No. Like I said, they're infinite.'

'Wow.'

I can see Dirk going all thoughtful. I imagine cogs and wheels and crankshafts in his brain turning and moving, and lights flashing on and off. Kind of a steampunk model of the brain. He doesn't say anything for a bit. Neither do I.

Then Dirk's like, 'So if this is true, you can prove it, right?'

'Yeah, sure. What do you want me to wish for?'

'Wish this pavement was made of rubber. With a space underneath so it'll bounce.'

That's typical Dirk, that is. He can't think of anything straightforward, like a sausage sandwich, can he.

'All right,' I go. 'I wish this pavement was made of rubber, with a space underneath so it'll bounce.'

And the next second, the pavement goes all springy under our feet, and we're bouncing along on it, *sproing sproing sproing*, like on a trampoline. There's an old lady walking her dog a bit further ahead, and she starts bouncing along too. She can't believe what's happening – she bends down to inspect the pavement, and the dog starts sniffing it.

Dirk looks at me. He's much too cool to show how amazed he is, of course. Dirk never loses his cool. He just raises his eyebrows in that quizzical way and goes 'Remarkable', like Mr Spock in the first *Star Trek* series.

'Yeah, good, innit.'

'What else can you do?'

'You name it.'

'So – you can have anything you want?'

'Yeah. Any requests?'

'Could you make us fly?'

'Course I could. I wish Dirk and me could fly.'

And then we take off – just go floating off the ground like a couple of helium balloons. It feels fantastic, I feel so light and free, I just can't help laughing aloud. Dirk's laughing too. He's like, 'Oh, man – this is unbelievable!'

We can change direction by flapping our arms, so we go swooping around, about five metres off the ground, dodging round the lamp-posts and trees. The wind's blowing through our hair and every time we catch each other's eye, we burst out laughing. It's like being little kids again.

The old lady with her dog is staring back at us, kind of tottering on her heels. She must think she's gone completely insane. And now there's a few other people coming along the road, there's a road sweeper with a cart and a woman pushing a buggy and a guy in a suit and tie coming home from work, and none of them know whether to stare down at the bouncy pavement under their feet or up at me and Dirk zooming around like a couple of swallows.

This makes us laugh at first, and I do this thing of swooping right down low over their heads to give them a fright – but it works too well, and they look really, like, panicked. The woman with the buggy screams and the kid in it starts crying, and they all start trying to run away on the bouncy pavement, but it's not easy to run on and they're bouncing around all over the place. And I start to feel kind of mean, wishing I hadn't scared them like that. So I'm like, 'I wish no one would take any notice of us,' – and the next minute, they're all just going about their business like nothing out of the ordinary's happened.

'Good call,' goes Dirk. 'You'd better put the pavement back to normal too.'

So I do, and then, feeling a bit tired after all the excitement, I'm like, 'Let's have a rest,' and I land on the roof of the nearest house. I'm sitting with my back to the chimney, and Dirk comes floating over to join me.

'Fancy a bag of chips?'

'Yeah, don't mind if I do.'

So I wish for two bags of chips and there they are in our hands, all hot and crisp and golden. The chips, I mean, not our hands. I wish for ketchup on mine, but Dirk has mayonnaise. He went to Brussels with his folks last year and ever since then he's always had mayonnaise on his chips, cause that's what they eat in Belgium.

You know, I reckon this was the first time I really appreciated the weirdness of what had happened. It was after five o'clock by now –

it wouldn't get properly dark for another half-hour or so, but already the sky was a deep blue, and behind the roofs of the houses opposite there was a kind of pink tinge – beautiful, if you go in for sunsets. And it was dead quiet, just a few people passing by in the street below, but they didn't look up at us of course, and somewhere a bird was singing. And there I was, sitting on the roof – on the roof! – with Dirk, eating chips that had been magicked up from nowhere, and thinking about all the weird stuff I'd done that day, and all the even weirder stuff there was still to do, and I felt, like, *poised* between the past and the future, you know?

Dirk's like, 'You know –' Then he stops, like he can't get the words out, and he purses up his lips like he's going to start whistling, but no sound comes out. 'Can you wish I could say that word again? The one you wished I'd stop saying?'

I can't work out what he's on about for a minute. 'What?'

'That's the one.'

'Oh, right! I wish you could say "what" again.'

'Thanks. I was just gonna say, do you know what you are?'

'What?' I go into defensive mode, thinking he's about to say something insulting.

'You're a god.'

'A god? What are you on about?'

'That's what you are, a god. You are. I mean, you could wish to be immortal, right?'

'Yeah, I spose I could, but I don't know if I wanna do that. I'd be living on and on when everyone else was dead, wouldn't I?'

'Yeah, but you could wish everyone else was immortal too.'

'Yeah, I spose I could, but I dunno if that's a good idea...'

'I'm not saying it is a good idea. I'm just saying, that's how much power you've got. You're a god, Adam.'

'Well... yeah, I spose I am a bit of a god, if you put it like that.' How about that, me being a god. 'What do you reckon I should wish for, then?'

'I dunno.' Dirk goes all thoughtful again. 'I reckon you need to think about it.'

'Yeah, I'm going to.'

'You gotta think really carefully. Cause you could do anything, man. You gotta think about the consequences…'

'I know that,' I say, a bit annoyed. I mean, I don't need lectures here. I'm the one with the wishes, right? 'Anyway, do you want me to wish for anything for you?'

'Dunno. Maybe. Let me think. I'll get back to you.'

'OK.'

Then we don't say anything for a while, just eat our chips, staring out over the rooftops.

Then Dirk's like, 'So – why aren't you going out with Natalie Forbes? You said that's what you'd wish for if you got the chance.'

'Yeah, well, I just haven't got round to it yet.'

I don't want to tell Dirk I've already tried this and it went tits-up. The story doesn't show me in a very good light, somehow. Makes me look sort of, well, a bit of a tosser, I suppose. 'I am gonna go out with her soon. I've got a plan.'

And I have. I've just thought of one.

I sat in my bedroom and looked at my face in the dressing-table mirror. It looked like it normally did. Just a face, you know. Two eyes and a nose and a mouth. Plus a few zits. But this was the face of a god. A god. I suddenly thought, it was ridiculous for a god to have to put up with zits. I mean, you don't hear of Zeus or Odin or any of those guys having zits. So I was like, 'I wish all my zits would go.'

I wasn't too badly off spot-wise at this time. I had a small one on my chin, but that was on its way out, and a big red one under my jaw, but that wasn't too bad because you couldn't really see it properly cause of where it was, and I had one just starting by the side of my nose, which didn't look too bad yet, but felt as if it was going to be a monster when it really got going. Anyway, anyway. In under a nanosecond, I didn't have any spots at all. They'd all gone. Vanished. Evaporated. My face was as clear as, I don't know, what's really clear, a field of snow or a skating rink or something. And it looked just fine.

But that was just the start, of course. The start of my plan for Natalie. OK, wishing she'd fall in love with me hadn't worked out the way I wanted. And I'd made the decision not to interfere with other people's emotions. But I wasn't about to give up on her. I *couldn't* give up on her. Being in love with Natalie was a condition that I was just stuck with, like, I don't know, asthma or something. In fact, it was quite similar to asthma, because thinking about Natalie made me short of breath. So, this was the plan. Instead of making wishes about *her*, I'd make wishes about *me*. I'd turn myself into such an amazing guy that she'd just have to fall in love with me. And this time it would be of her own accord.

So, next I'm like, 'I wish I was six foot two.' This seemed like a pretty cool height to be – it's not tall enough to be a freak, but it's pretty impressive for someone who's only just turned seventeen.

I felt my back and legs stretching out. It was kind of weird, but quite a pleasant feeling. And there I was, six foot two.

I got up and walked over to the full-length mirror on the wardrobe door to get a better look. And then I was like, 'Oh, for Christ's sake!'

What's happened is, I've got longer legs and a longer body, but the rest of me is the same as before, so it's all out of proportion. I'm too skinny for my height, my arms hardly dangle down as far as my waist, and my head looks way too small, like an apple stuck on top of a telegraph pole.

I could see I'd have to work on this. 'I wish I was all in proportion, like before.' Instantly, the proportions altered. I was pleased with what I saw – now that my head was bigger I looked older, a man not a boy. It's something I've noticed, by the way, that people who get on in life, the ones who reach the top, headmasters or football managers or politicians or CEOs and stuff, usually have massive heads, like pumpkins or beach balls or great blocks of granite. I don't know why. Perhaps people take you more seriously if you've got a large head because they think it must be full of brains. So I was pretty glad to have one.

I looked OK now, but I thought I might as well make myself a bit more handsome. I mean, why not? So I was like, 'I wish I had a square chin.' And a second later, for the second time, 'Oh, for Christ's sake!' Cause I've been given a *completely* square chin, totally geometric, like it's been drawn with a ruler. It looks hideous. He's having a laugh, that genie, I reckon. So I was like, 'Not totally square, you moron. I wish it was a bit squarer than before, but it's still gotta look like a human chin, all right?'

This time around it looks fine. So then I really get to work, mod-elling myself into the hunkiest man in the universe. It's really weird, watching myself morph into something different in the mirror. It takes a long time, cause the genie tends to take things a bit too liter-ally and I have to keep fine-tuning it. But when I looked at the fin-ished result, I just thought, 'Wow!' I mean, if I was a girl, or gay, I'd fancy me. I'd given myself a six-pack of steel, and I'd made my chest broader, and my biceps bigger and my thighs thicker, so now you'd look at me and go, Whoa, that guy's really built! And as well as the square but not-totally-square chin, I'd given myself a pair of those high cheekbones that male models in fashion mags have. Another thing I'd done was to give myself jet-black hair – it used to be mousy brown. My eyes used to be a sort of browny colour too, but now I'd made them green – bright green, like a cat's. I reckoned this would appeal to Natalie, cause her eyes were green, too – not as bright as mine, though – and I thought she might go for a guy with the same eye colour as her, it would be like a sort of connection between us. Of course if it turned out she didn't like green eyes in guys, I'd change them to blue, or back to brown, or whatever she liked best. She could have purple if she wanted.

So, what else could I do, apart from change the way I looked? Well, girls like guys with money, right? I mean, whatever they say, they do. Natalie had been dead impressed when I'd got rid of the parkie by chucking money at him. Of course, she'd been in love with me at the time cause of my wish, but she'd still remember it, and a few more gestures like that should convince her that I was a) loaded and b) generous – and what girl could resist that combina-tion? I decided a thousand would do to be going on with. After all I could always wish for more when it ran out. So I was like, 'I wish I had a thousand squid'.

And just the very second I've said the words, I think 'That was a big mistake.'

But it's too late now.

There's a sort of sickening squelching sound, and the room is full of slimy slithering squids. They're on the bed, on the carpet, on the dressing table, on top of the wardrobe, pale gloopy creatures with astonished eyes and twitching tentacles. It must have given them quite a fright, suddenly materialising in my bedroom, cause they start squirting out all that black ink stuff, making a terrible mess everywhere. There's a strong smell too, a sort of squiddy sea smell.

And I think, thank God I didn't wish for a million squid. If I had, I'd probably have been squashed, smothered, flattened, suffocated by them.

And what a sad, pathetic way to die that would have been – killed by squids when the world was my oyster.

'Who the hell are you? What are you doing here?'

My dad jumps up from his chair, nearly knocking his beer over. His hands grip the edge of the table. My mum looks scared, and Emily starts to cry.

'It's me, innit? Who do you think it is?'

But they're still staring at me blankly. My dad picks up the phone. 'I'm calling the police,' he goes. 'You'd better get out of here. Don't you try anything. I was a judo expert in my youth. I did judo for the county.'

Then I get it. He doesn't recognise me. None of them recognise me. They think I'm a burglar or something. I should have anticipated this. I don't know why I didn't think of it. Those squids must have destroyed my focus.

I'm like, 'I wish you recognised me.'

Immediately they all look relieved. Emily stops crying and starts smiling, like the sun coming out after the rain. Dad sits down again. And Mum's like, 'Adam – what have you done to yourself?'

I don't want to get into a load of explanations here, so I'm like, 'I wish you thought I'd always been tall and handsome with black hair and green eyes and no zits, in fact I wish everyone who knew me thought that, so no one will notice I look different, but they'll notice

I look cool, of course, only they won't realise it's a new thing, is that OK?'

The last bit was addressed to the genie. I didn't get a direct answer, but the wish seemed to work. Mum and Dad and Emily kind of lost interest in me. Emily started playing with a bit of tinfoil she'd found on the carpet and Mum and Dad carried on with an argument they'd been having about one of Dad's pupils who'd complained he smelled of drink. Mum was saying Dad had better cut down on the drink or he'd be out of a job and Dad was saying Mum (who was halfway through a bottle of white) was a fine one to talk.

I'm like, 'I wish you two would kiss and make up.'

So they do, and Emily laughs and claps her hands and we're all like one big happy family. For the moment.

'Here, Em, I've got something for you.' It's a big doll, almost as big as Emily, of Riley out of *Inside Out*. I wished for it on the way downstairs. I produce it from behind my back.

'Fanks Adam! It's bee-yoo-tiful.' She grabs the doll and starts wrapping its head in tinfoil.

'I'm off out, OK?'

'All right,' goes Mum. 'Don't be late for supper, will you? We've got calamari tonight.'

I'm feeling cool as I set off for Natalie's. Cause, yeah, that's what I've decided, to go right round and ask her out again. And this time I won't need to wish she loves me, because how can she say no? I look like a film star, I'm a genius at probability, I'm in the school football team and I beat the crap out of Steve Renwick. Plus I've got a thousand quid in my pocket.

Natalie's house is in a big, posh road where all the houses are different from each other. Much posher than my road. But then, her parents are posher than mine. And richer. They both have jobs that are something to do with the telly. They're producers. Whatever that means. I did once ask Natalie and she said, 'They make programmes', but I still didn't get what they actually *do*. I didn't like to ask her to explain in case she thought I was thick.

As I knock on the door, I can't help remembering Saturday, and

Natalie's wicked little smile and the way she looked standing there in her underwear. And the memory's so intense, I'm almost surprised when the door opens and she's standing there fully clothed.

'Hi, Natalie!'

Natalie looks surprised. 'Oh. Hi. I thought you were Claire.'

'Claire? Why would you think that? I don't look like her, do I?'

'No, only I'm expecting her.'

'Oh, right.' Why doesn't she ask me in? But she's standing right in the middle of the doorway, with her hand on the doorframe, like some sort of bouncer. Obviously, she doesn't want me to get any ideas about a re-run of Saturday being on the cards.

'I just sort of, you know, popped round, to see if you were up for another game of tennis.'

'But it's dark.'

'Oh, yeah, I didn't mean tonight, I just meant, you know, whenever you feel like it. Like tomorrow, say. Or Wednesday. Or any day, you know, I mean there's seven to choose from, isn't there?'

I realise I'm babbling, but I can't stop myself. 'Course, it doesn't have to be tennis. There's plenty of other stuff we can do, you know what I mean?' Then I realise that this sounds a bit pervy, and I honestly didn't mean it to, I swear. I can feel my face turning bright scarlet. 'Like, you know, we could go, er, *riding* or something.' Why did I say that? I'm sounding pervier and pervier. And I've never been riding in my life. I don't know what made me think of it.

'Let's leave it for the time being, shall we?'

I don't like that 'shall we', as if she's made some kind of really appealing suggestion I'm supposed to agree to, when in fact she's giving me the brush-off. *Shall we.* It's patronising, isn't it? Like I'm supposed to go, 'Yeah, what a great idea.' Then again, she did say 'for the time being'. Does that mean anything? Does it mean she's thinking about it and reckons she might change her mind in the future? But most probably she just put it in to soften the blow. Or probably not even that, it's just an expression, it means nothing at all. She's given me the brush-off, that's all there is to it. I feel gutted. Literally, like a fish that's just had its guts ripped out with a sharp knife.

I'm like, 'Yeah, whatever.' There's a kind of awkward pause. Then I go, 'I won the fight with Renwick.'

'Oh, did you?'

'Yeah, I beat the crap out of him.'

But for some reason Natalie doesn't look very impressed by this. She's like, 'Good for you', but she doesn't sound like she thinks there's anything very good about it. There's another of those awkward kind of pauses.

'Well… yeah… I'd better be off, then.'

'Right. Bye then.'

And the front door swings closed, and there I am left standing on the doorstep like a lemon. I stand there looking at the door for a bit. It's a bright red one, one with a shiny gleaming knocker.

At the top of the road, just as I'm turning the corner, I almost bump into Claire.

'Hi, Adam!'

'Hi.'

I've always liked Claire. I mean, I don't fancy her in particular, but she's always been very friendly to me. And she's got a good sense of humour. She laughs at my jokes. I've always had the feeling that she kind of likes me, in fact.

I stop and look at her now, and I think, she doesn't look too bad. Actually quite nice. A bit dumpy, maybe, but that's not a crime, is it? She's got one of those sort of round faces with straight fair hair in a kind of helmet shape around it. Grey eyes. Nice smile.

'I'm just going round to Natalie's.'

'Yeah, I know.' I suddenly feel a little pang of envy for Claire, for being Natalie's best friend. In a minute she'll be up in Natalie's bedroom, chatting and giggling away, sitting on the bed. While I'll be slouching along the street, wondering what to do with myself. It's just – I mean, it's just not fair, is it?

And I bet they talk about me, too.

'Give her my –' Then I stop. I'd been about to say, 'Give her my love,' but then I thought that's maybe overdoing it a bit, so I thought about changing it to, 'Give her my kind regards,' but then I think maybe that sounds a bit sarcastic. So then it comes out all wrong, of course, and I end up saying, 'Give her my loving regards'.

'Your what?'

'My loving regards.' I feel a bit annoyed with her for making me repeat it. 'What's the matter – haven't you heard that expression before?'

'No.'

I'm like, 'It's in common usage,' but it doesn't sound totally convincing. I can't think of anything to say after that, so I just go, 'Well, see you around then,' and go slouching off. And as she goes walking off round the corner I sort of half get the impression that she's laughing. I like it when I make her laugh but only if that was the intention. I wonder what she'll say to Natalie about it.

'I wish I was a fly on the wall in Natalie's bedroom,' I go, just muttering it, not really meaning to make a wish. But the next second, that's exactly what and where I was.

You've probably never been a fly before, so I'd better explain what it's like. Obviously, the first thing you notice is how small you are. Just a little speck. But I didn't feel weak – I felt small and sassy, like I wouldn't take any shit from anyone. I was a dirty little horrible fly and nobody liked me and I didn't give a toss, that's how I felt. Like I was a little devil, or imp, or something, you know what I mean? I went zooming around Natalie's room, changing direction with a twitch of my wings, making this cool buzzing noise like I was a miniature light aircraft. I zoomed past the posters on the walls and the Penguin Classics and buzzed round the dragon made of sea-shells and the china unicorn on the dressing table. It all looked different, cause I had these big goggly compound eyes that broke everything up into little overlapping squares. It was cool. And I understood why flies spend so much of their time pointlessly buzzing round. It's just for the sheer fun of it.

The door opened and Natalie came in with Claire. They each had a cup of tea and Natalie was carrying a plate of biscuits. More than I got offered, I thought with a pang of bitterness. I got offered nothing.

Natalie sat down on a big pink beanbag. Even seen through compound eyes, all broken up into little overlapping squares, she still looked totally gorgeous.

Claire sat on the bed. She sipped her tea and crunched a Garibaldi. 'I like these. Squashed fly biscuits, my mum calls them.'

I didn't like the sound of that. I landed high on the wall and kept very still. I didn't want them noticing me and trying to swat me with a magazine or something. I mean, just imagine that, getting squashed by a magazine wielded by the girl you love. It's what you'd call a tragic end.

Natalie's like, 'If you could only eat three types of biscuits ever again, what would they be?'

'Ooh, well, let's say I'll keep the squashed fly ones in there. Then maybe... Bourbons? And Jaffa cakes.'

'The question is whether Jaffa cakes count as biscuits.'

'Of course they're biscuits!'

'Why aren't they called Jaffa Biscuits, then?'

They both laughed at this, although it didn't strike me as especially funny. Then they started talking about the English homework that Miss Rogers had just set. An essay on the *Great Gatsby*. In what ways is it a critique of the American dream? (Actually they came up with some pretty good ideas I thought I might be able to use myself.) And after that Natalie started talking about an exhibition of surrealist art on the South Bank she'd heard about and wanted to go and see and they started making plans about when they could go. I started to get a bit frustrated. They say eavesdroppers never hear good of themselves but I wasn't hearing anything about myself at all. They were ignoring me completely!

But that was about to change.

Claire was like, 'Guess who I met outside?'

'Idris Elba.'

They cackle like hyenas for a bit.

'No,' Claire says eventually. 'I met Adam.'

'Oh, did you?' Natalie didn't sound too interested, I have to say.

'He sent you his loving regards.'

'His what?'

'That's what he said, his loving regards. He said it was in common usage.'

Natalie tapped her head kinda significantly. 'He's out to lunch, that boy, I reckon.' Then they both start laughing. Laughing. At me. I mean, what a cheek. And Claire's a fine one to laugh, anyway. She's always getting expressions wrong.

'He's not playing with a full deck,' goes Natalie.

'He's got a marble loose!' goes Claire.

'No, that's a screw loose. Or lost his marbles.'

'Whatever!' goes Claire and they both scream with laughter again.

'He was round here just now, you know,' goes Natalie after they've calmed down.

'Was he? What did he want?'

'Wanted to play tennis again.'

'What did you say?'

'Said no, of course. I mean, after last time…'

Then they both laugh again. Madly. Like hyenas who've just inhaled a load of nitrous oxide.

'I dunno, though. Why don't you say yes?' goes Claire after a bit. 'I mean, he is pretty gorgeous. I wouldn't say no.'

I'm starting to like her more and more.

'You've got to admit he's good-looking,' goes Claire. And I'm thinking, right, that's right, tell it like it is.

'He looks OK, I suppose,' goes Natalie. 'If you like that sort of look. But he's so annoying. He really reckons himself, and he's always trying to make people laugh, and he's just not funny.'

That is simply not true. I'm really good at making people laugh. It's the only thing I *am* any good at. I'm always making Emily laugh.

'Oh, I think he's funny sometimes,' goes Claire. 'He can be quite a laugh.'

'No, he's too self-conscious, he tries too hard. I think there's something a bit sort of… embarrassing about him.'

Embarrassing! How dare she say that about me? I don't why I'm staying here listening to this. I didn't come here to be insulted. I feel like just buzzing off. But I know I can't, I have to stay here and hear this out, it's like I'm pinned to the wall.

'I think he's really all right, you know,' goes Claire loyally.

But Natalie shakes her head and kind of screws up her face. 'Not my type.'

'Isn't he? Who is your type, then? Apart from Idris Elba!'

Natalie hesitates for a moment and then she's like, 'Dirk Hudson.'

Dirk Hudson.

That's what she said.

That's just the last bleeding straw. My best mate. Dirk. When I heard this, I felt – how can I explain it? I felt like I had a great big juicy red heart, like you see on Valentine cards, and it had just been pierced right to the centre with a long pin. Or with a dirk. I remember Dirk telling me that his name meant some kind of dagger they used in Scotland. They used to keep them in their socks, in the days of the Highland clans. Well, I'd just been stabbed with one. A big sharp long one. And I felt like I was bleeding to death.

Slowly, I began to creep down the wall towards the door. I mean, I just wanted to get out of there now. But I didn't want to fly and buzz and draw attention to myself. No, I just wanted to creep quietly away. I didn't feel like a sassy, don't-give-a-toss, take-no-crap fly any more. I felt small and weak, a fragile little creature that could be crushed with a single blow.

And in a way, I just had been.

All the time I was creeping towards the door, Natalie and Claire carried on talking. About Dirk.

'So... would you?' Claire asked.

'Would I what?'

Claire giggled. 'You know.'

And Natalie gave that wicked little smile again. The one she'd once bestowed upon me. She was like, 'I might. I just might.'

It just wasn't decent, the way she said it. She was practically licking her lips. I don't think girls should talk like that. It's a disgrace, if you want my opinion.

Well, I got to the door at last and I crawled under it – and then I flew down the stairs and into the hall. There was a sort of stained glass window thing at the top of the front door and it was open, so I zoomed through it and out into the street. I was like, 'I wish I was human again' in a little squeaky fly voice. And there I was, standing on the pavement, all six foot two of me.

Then I made another wish.

'I wish Dirk Hudson never hooks up with Natalie Forbes.'

Yeah, I know. It wasn't very nice of me. But I wasn't feeling very nice. I mean, what do you expect?

I might be a god, but I'm only human.

CHAPTER 4

'Come on you O's!'

There was a deafening roar as the team ran out on the pitch – no, only kidding. You don't get deafening roars at Orient. The crowd only averages about five thousand, and this game was a midweek one so it was even less. But there was a kind of loud murmur as the team ran out on the pitch. The opposition tonight was Ebbsfleet, a fairly crap team, but Orient have this habit of getting turned over by crap teams. We needed to win this one because, as usual, we were locked in a relegation battle. It's the same every bloody year, of course. We start out with high hopes and the Chairman always writes stuff in the programme about how this season, at last, we'll get promoted back into the professional league. But by the time Christmas has been and gone he's changed his tune and he's writing stuff about how this year, once again, we'll avoid relegation.

I'd been coming to the O's with Dirk for about two years. It was him who got me into it. Before that, I'd supported Arsenal, mainly because it was Martin Bone's team and we were good friends at primary school. Martin's a massive Arsenal fan and it's his ambition to play for them. But he hardly ever actually went to games because from the age of twelve onwards he was always playing football himself on Saturdays, for a youth team called Woodford Wanderers over on Hackney Marshes. So I didn't go either. I was pretty much a casual supporter. I knew the names of all the team and I watched them on 'Match of the Day' and stuff. But I never actually went to the Emirates. It was too far and my dad never wanted to take me. He doesn't like watching football. That's what he says, anyway. In fact he doesn't mind watching it on the telly with a few beers. If he went to the ground he'd have to sit there for two hours without a drink, that's what it is.

Anyway, I liked Arsenal cause they were a London side and they'd won plenty of stuff, and even when they didn't win stuff they were always kind of in the frame for winning stuff. But then one day Dirk persuaded me to go to the O's with him. And I kind of liked it. The ground was close enough so we could walk there, and it was a small ground, not too crowded, and there was a good-natured atmosphere – everyone wanted the team to win, but didn't really expect them to, and forgave them when they didn't.

'It's better to support your local team,' Dirk said. 'There's no point supporting some team that's miles away just cause they're successful. If that's all you care about, you might as well support Barcelona or Bayern Munich or someone. Don't you reckon?'

'I spose.' I'd never really thought of it like that.

'Of course, Orient aren't doing too well this season, but so what? If there's no bad times, you don't appreciate the good times.'

Two seasons later, I was starting to wonder whether there'd ever be any good times to appreciate at Orient. But I still kept going along. It had got to be a bit of a habit.

'Do you reckon we'll win today?' goes Dirk, as they kicked off.

'Yeah, I reckon we'll win 10–0.'

Dirk laughs. 'Yeah, right.'

'No, seriously. I guarantee it.'

Dirk looked at me. 'You haven't, have you?'

'Wait and see!'

'What d'you go and wish for a thing like that for?' He sounded annoyed.

'Wodjer mean, what's wrong with wishing for it? *You* wish they'd win, don't you?'

'Yeah, but I know the wish isn't gonna come true.'

'So it's all the better if it does come true, innit?'

'No! Look, the whole point is, they have to do it themselves!'

'Well, they'll do it themselves, won't they? Look!'

Sammy Pollock, one of Orient's most talentless players, had just hoofed the ball aimlessly upfield. It landed in the Ebbsfleet penalty area, took an awkward bounce and skidded past the keeper into the net. Pollock went wild, jumping around and punching the air. The crowd cheered. All except Dirk.

'This is just silly,' he goes. 'What's the point of watching when you know the result already?'

'You can enjoy seeing the O's win.'

'Yeah, but it doesn't *mean* anything.'

I didn't argue any more. I just settled down to watch the game. It turned out to be pretty funny. Cause I hadn't wished that Orient would play any better than usual, you see. I'd only wished for the result. So they got the goals, but they were all flukes. A freak gust of wind, a dodgy penalty decision, a disastrous own goal, an inexplicable goalkeeping error – all this kind of stuff went against Ebbsfleet – while at the other end, Orient's goal seemed to be protected by a sort of invisible force field. Funnily enough, Ebbsfleet were playing pretty well, passing the ball about nicely, having most of the possession. But they still went in at half-time five goals down.

'I've had enough of this,' Dirk goes. 'I'm going home.'

He got up and walked out. I was going to let him go, then I changed my mind and ran after him. I caught him up outside in Brisbane Road.

'Look, what's the matter?'

'That wasn't a game of football, was it? It was a joke.'

'Yeah, it was pretty funny –'

'Football's not supposed to be funny!'

'OK, but that was my first attempt. In future, I can wish for better games. Closer ones. More exciting.'

'You're not getting it, are you? There has to be some tension – some uncertainty – that's the whole point of football. If you've fixed the game in advance, well…' He shrugged. 'There's just no point, is there?'

'Well… maybe you're right.' I didn't want to argue about it. And he did have a point. After all, if I'd thought the second half was worth staying for, I'd have stayed for it. 'Look, I won't fix any more games, OK?'

We walked on in silence for a bit. Then I was like, 'Have you thought of anything you want me to wish for? You can have anything you like.'

'I've thought about it. But… I dunno. I was kinda thinking of getting you to wish I knew more – that I could answer all these, like, philosophical questions and stuff. You know, like wish I knew if there's free will, or if God exists, or what the purpose of life is.'

'OK, you got it.' Typical Dirk, I'm thinking, to wish to be even more of a know-all than he already is.

'No, but then I decided not to. Cause – well, you have to find stuff out for yourself, don't you?'

'Do you?'

'Well, stuff always means more when you've had to get it yourself, doesn't it?'

'I dunno.'

'It's like…' He stops and thinks for a bit. 'Look, why haven't you wished that Natalie was your girlfriend yet?'

'Well, I dunno, really…'

'It's cause you want to get her to choose you herself, isn't? You don't want it to happen just cause you've wished it.'

He's pretty sharp, sometimes, Dirk.

'Yeah, I spose.' I felt a twinge of guilt, thinking about Natalie. If I'd let her choose for herself she'd be going out with Dirk. I didn't feel proud of that. But I wasn't about to unwish it. I'd just make sure that no one ever found out.

I decided to change the subject. 'Nice day today, isn't it?' We'd had yet another bright, sunny, advance instalment on spring, and even though the sun was getting low now, it was still pretty warm for late afternoon in February.

'Yeah, lovely.'

'Glad you like it. I ordered it specially.'

Dirk looked at me. 'You didn't, did you?'

'I did.'

'You wanna be careful, man. Haven't you heard of the butterfly effect?'

I was like, 'Course I have.' I'm bluffing, of course. I haven't got a clue what the butterfly effect is. It sounds like it could be the name of a band, I suppose.

'Yeah? What is it, then?'

'It's – er…' Suddenly, I get an inspiration. 'I know, it's that painting thing kids do in primary school, when you get a bit of paper and you slosh paint on one side of it and fold it over, and it looks like a butterfly. That's it, innit?'

'No, you moron. The butterfly effect is a term from chaos theory. It says that if a butterfly flaps its wings it can cause a hurricane.'

This makes me laugh. 'Have to be a pretty massive butterfly.'

'No, just an ordinary butterfly. It flaps its wings and that causes a tiny bit of air turbulence, and that displaces a bit more air, and that causes a bit more turbulence, and it all builds up till in the end you get a hurricane.'

This theory sounds like bollocks to me.

I'm like, 'That's bollocks. Butterflies are flapping their wings all the time, that's all they ever do, it's how they get around. So why aren't we all being constantly flattened with hurricanes?'

'It doesn't say it *always* causes a hurricane, you moron. There's lots of other factors, right, too many to calculate. It just says in certain conditions it *can* cause a hurricane. That's why you have to be careful with the weather. You can't calculate what the knock-on effect is gonna be if you change anything.'

'So?'

'These sunny days you're wishing for – they might end up causing a flood in Thailand or a tornado in Arizona or something.'

'So what? I've got my wishes, haven't I? I could wish for the flood or the tornado to go away again.'

'Yeah, but then you don't know what the effect of *that* would be. There's always, you know, consequences. That's why you can't just go around doing what you like, being a hedonist.'

I'm like, 'A what?' I'm getting a tiny bit fed up with Dirk lecturing me. If 'hedonist' turns out to be another word for 'moron', he's going to be sorry. I'm thinking of wishing for a small black raincloud to hover just above his head and piss down with rain on him all the way home.

'A hedonist is someone who lives for pleasure alone.'

'Sounds like a good plan to me.'

'No it isn't. It's a flawed philosophy.'

'Is it though?'

'Yes. If you live for pleasure alone, you end up getting less happiness than if you've got lots of different aims in life. It's having the aims, working towards them, that's what makes life worthwhile. So hedonism doesn't really do what it says on the tin.'

'Doesn't it?'

'No.'

'Right,' I go. 'Well, we'll see about that, shall we? I wish I had a Porsche turbo 511. A silver one, please.'

Instantly, it materialised at the roadside. A beautiful, gleaming, silver machine. I opened the door.

'Get in, Dirk. I'll give you a lift home.'

Dirk's goggling at the Porsche in amazement. 'But – you can't drive.'

'Oh, yeah. Soon fix that. I wish I could drive.'

We got in. I closed the door. It made a kind of solid, satisfying thunk.

'OK – I wish I didn't crash, or knock anyone over, or have any kind of accident, or get stopped by the cops no matter how fast I drive. Let's go!'

I turned the key. The engine throbbed into life. I put my foot down. The car roared down Leyton High Road. In five seconds the speedo needle was reading sixty and rising fast. I kept my foot down, dodging in and out of the slow-moving traffic.

'I wish we had some music playing – 'Lighting Strikes Twice' by The Jaguar Smile.'

The sounds of 'Lightning Strikes Twice' filled the car. Loud and clear. It was cool.

'I wish I had an ice cream,' I yelled. 'And one for Dirk too!'

Dirk was like, 'Thanks. But you just jumped a red light!'

'So what?' As I said it, I got this kind of thrill, a sort of tingle deep down in my guts. I could say 'so what' and mean it now, in any situation. It wasn't just, like, bravado. I really and truly *did not have to give a toss about anything.*

I was free.

The speedo touched eighty.

'Let's get out in the country and take it to the max!'

We got clear of Leyton High Road and turned up Lea Bridge Road, heading out Essex way.

I got another idea.

'I wish the glove compartment was full of twenty-pound notes. Go on, Dirk, help yourself.'

Dirk opened the glove compartment. Neat bundles of twenties tumbled out onto the floor. Dirk was like, 'Wow!' He started picking them up and putting them in his pockets. 'Thanks, man!'

'That's OK. Not too bad, this hedonism lark, is it?'

For once, Dirk didn't seem too sure of himself. He looked a bit kind of shamefaced and mumbled something about money always coming in handy.

The speedo touched ninety.

We left London behind. Through Woodford Green, on towards High Beach, rushing through Epping Forest. The trees went flickering past.

The speedo touched a hundred.

I couldn't help laughing from sheer exhilaration. I reckoned I'd been under-using my wishes so far. But Dirk had put me on the right track with his talk about hedonism. Living for pleasure alone. That was it. Way to go. I was going to live for pleasure alone from here on in.

The speedo touched 120.

For some reason, I thought of Claire.

CHAPTER 5

'Hey, Claire! Wanna lift home?'

'Adam!' Claire stared at me, sitting in my silver Porsche with the window open and my elbow resting casually on the sill. She'd just come out of school carrying her bag in one hand and her violin in the other. She always had her violin lesson on a Thursday after school. It was quarter past four and everyone else had gone home. Everyone else except me.

'Jump in.'

'But – but...' She was half amazed and half-grinning. The thing about Claire is, she has an incredibly expressive face. When she has an emotion her face registers it, big-time. She'd have been a great silent movie star. 'What a fantastic car! It's not yours, is it?'

'Sure it's mine. Got it in a cracker at Christmas.'

'But – you can't drive it, can you?'

'Get in and find out.'

'When did you pass your test? You were only 17 last month, weren't you?'

'You're as old as you feel, that's what my old granny always says. And she's just run away to join the circus!'

'Has she really?'

'Course she has. Get in.'

Claire's face went into a sort of comically nervous expression with her eyes wide and her lower lip turned down. 'You're sure it's... all right?'

'Look, you don't want to walk home in the rain, do you?'

Claire made the sort of face that signified, as clearly as if she'd said it aloud, *Well-OK-then-this-may-be-a-bit crazy-but-what-the-hell,* and she came round the other side of the car and got in.

I drove away smoothly and slowly. I had a feeling Claire wouldn't be impressed by speeding. I set the windscreen wipers going in a nice steady rhythm – it was drizzling slightly, cause I'd stopped wishing for sunny days after what Dirk had said about the butterfly effect. I mean, it was probably bollocks, but I didn't want to have to start sorting out the whole world's climate, just in case it turned out not to be bollocks.

'How was the lesson?'

'Oh, it was OK.'

'Yeah? I used to have violin lessons. Then I decided it was a bit of a fiddle.'

'Did you? Oh –!' She laughed, getting the joke. I liked the way her face lit up when she laughed. I knew she didn't really think it was funny – I mean, no one could think a crap joke like that was funny – but she was laughing to be friendly, and I liked that. In fact, I felt more at ease with Claire than I did with Natalie. I didn't fancy her as much – if, say, I fancied Natalie 100%, then Claire was about 65% – but maybe that was the reason I felt more at ease with her. Maybe it's better to go out with someone you only fancy a reasonable amount. Then you can relax a bit more. Plus, I knew Claire thought I was gorgeous, because I'd heard her say it in Natalie's bedroom. So that kind of helped.

I looked down at her legs. Plump knees, but that was OK. In fact they were pretty nice knees. Maybe I fancied her a bit more than 65%. Maybe it was more like 70%.

'Hey, Claire?'

'Yes?' She looked at me with her nice grey eyes, all kind of full of bright, friendly interest.

'Wanna go out some time?'

'Love to!'

I feel a little warm buzz at this. If it had been Natalie, it would have felt more like a nuclear bomb exploding inside me, but a warm buzz is OK to be going on with.

'Well, that was the right answer, Claire! And your reward is a hot date, with me.'

'Sounds nice. Where are we going to go?'

'Wait and see, Claire. Wait and see!'

I give her a kiss when I drop her off – just lip-to-cheek, you know. 'See you tomorrow night, then.'

'OK!'

'Pick you up about eight?'

'I can't wait!'

'I won't be late!'

'Great!'

We're getting along pretty well with the rhymes here, like a couple of rappers, but now I can't think of another word to keep it going, except for 'salivate' and that doesn't seem quite suitable. Then a few more words ending in '-ate' pop into my head, but they're even less suitable. So I just say, 'Good night', and watch her trot up the path to her front door, looking pretty pleased, if you can judge by the back view.

And I'm feeling pretty pleased, too, as I drive off. I've got a date tomorrow.

And I didn't even have to wish for it.

We went to the cinema, to see a film with Seth Rogen in. As we were going into the cinema, I was like, 'Imagine if his first name was Josh.'

'Why?'

'Then he'd sound like a backwards curry!'

Claire giggled about this all the way through the ads and the trailers. I thought it was pretty cool to be going out with someone who appreciated my sense of humour so much.

It was a pretty boring film, in my opinion. It was a kind of comedy-thriller. Seth Rogen goes to Las Vegas with some system he's got to break the bank, and he meets this girl he falls in love with, but she's a gambler too and she says she's also got a system and she wins more than he does, but then she gets kidnapped by these villains and they threaten to torture her if she doesn't tell them the system. The thing is she hasn't even really got a system, she was just bragging to Seth Rogen and the villains overheard and then she went and won by sheer dumb luck. Anyway, Seth Rogen rescues her in the end. There's this scene where he has to play Russian roulette with the villains and they all blow their brains out except him. The girl asks him how he did it and he reveals that that was sheer dumb luck too. That was the title of the film, *Sheer Dumb Luck*. They could have just left out the first and third words, in my opinion. It was kind of an implausible story.

But there was one good bit. This was when, just after the last villain has blasted his head off in the game of Russian roulette, Seth Rogen turns to the camera and goes, 'I hear that Adam Gowers is in the cinema tonight with his beautiful new girlfriend, Claire. Raise your hand and give us a wave, buddy!'

I raised my hand. I gave a wave.

Seth Rogen waved back. 'Yeah, there they are, right there in the middle row. How's it goin', buddy? Hope you're enjoying the movie! Wishin' ya all the best.'

Everyone's, like, looking round at me, completely amazed. And Claire's staring at me like I'm from Mars. She's like, 'What – what's going on?'

'Oh, nothing. Seth's an old mate of mine. His idea of a joke, I guess.'

'An old mate of yours?'

'Yeah, I, er – I met him on holiday once. In Devon. We got on like a house on fire. He's a great laugh.'

'But – how could that scene get in the film? I mean – how did he – it doesn't make sense!'

She looks so bewildered and a little terrified. Well, I guess it was kind of freaky. No one's watching the film now, they're all looking at me as if I've just grown an extra head. I don't know what to do. I don't want to explain about the wishes to Claire, and I can't think of any other explanation. So in the end I'm like, 'I wish everyone would forget what just happened.'

Claire's like, 'What? What just happened?'

'Wodjer mean? Nothing happened. Watch the film.'

Everyone turned round again and settled down to watch the end of the film. Shame, really. I've always wanted something like that to happen, something impossible and weird and completely inexplicable. I thought it would make everyone think I was a really special person. But in real life people don't like freaky stuff. It freaks them out.

We came out of the cinema giggling at the stupid ending of the film. I made my joke about how they could have left out the first and third words of the title and Claire thought that was really witty.

'Hungry?'

Claire's like, 'I could eat a wolf!'

'Don't you mean horse?'

'Whatever.'

'I'll see what I can do.'

We ate out at a dead expensive restaurant in Wanstead. I ordered champagne, which made Claire even gigglier, even though she only had one glass. When I pretended to be looking for Roast Horse on the menu, she nearly wet herself. I felt like Oscar Wilde or someone. We did him for GCSE with Miss Rogers in English. *The Importance of Being Ernest.* I didn't think it was as funny as it was cracked up to be, quite frankly. I certainly didn't remember Claire laughing at it the way she was laughing at my jokes tonight. I decided that I did fancy her quite a lot, really.

Call it 75%.

Claire was like, 'I've never met anyone like you, Adam.'

'Haven't you?'

'You're still at school – but you drive a Porsche and order champagne in restaurants! I mean, how do you do it?'

'I'm just an amazing guy, that's all.'

'And so modest!'

I'm like, 'Yeah, I'm probably the most modest person the world has ever known.' This makes her laugh again.

'Would you care to order, sir?' That was the waiter, obviously.

I had steak and Claire chose a fillet of sole in some sort of sauce. She said it was really nice. I was like, 'Let's go home,' as she was spooning up the last of her creme caramel. I left a massive tip, of course. Out in the night air, I realised I was a bit wobbly from the champagne so I wished I was stone cold sober immediately.

We got in the car. The doors went clunk! Clunk! And we were away.

'How about inviting me in for cocoa and biscuits?' I say when we pull up outside her place. That line comes from a Noddy book I remember my dad reading me as a kid. Noddy says it to Big Ears. I always liked that line. It was kind of funny to think of me using it all those years later as a sort of seduction line.

'Yes, come in,' said Claire, sounding pleased. 'We'll have to be careful not to wake my parents, though. They'll be in bed by now.'

Oh, yeah, the parents. I'd better do something about them. While Claire was opening the front door, I quickly wished they'd gone out to spend the night at a hotel and left a note for Claire telling her so.

'They've gone out to spend the night at a hotel!' said Claire in amazement, picking the note up from the kitchen table.

'What a surprise. So we've got the house to ourselves.'

'Yes, completely to ourselves.'

'We're all alone.'

'No one to disturb us.'

'That's right.'

'Just you and me.'

Claire's standing really close to me, looking up into my face. I can smell her perfume, or shampoo or whatever it is. It's nice, kind of fruity. She looks really sweet and adorable. Her cheeks are flushed and her eyes are wide and her pupils are dilated. And I just think, like, *Wow*. Our faces approach each other as if they're magnetised – and then our mouths clamp together.

It was pretty cool. After a bit, we both kind of came up for air. She looked at me steadily with her nice wide grey eyes. She was like, 'Wow, I can't believe this is happening!'

'Me neither.'

'You could have any girl you wanted! Why choose me?'

''Cause you're the girl I want.'

'Really?'

'Yeah, really.'

'Really and truly?'

'Really and truly.' I felt a twinge of guilt saying this, cause obviously I'd rather have had Natalie given the chance. But what can you do? To bring the conversation to an end, I kissed her again.

After a bit, we graduated to the sofa, and things started to get more intense. I breathed into Claire's ear: 'Do you want to... you know?'

'Have you got any – you know?'

Got any? What was she talking about? Then I understood. 'I wish I had some condoms – oh yeah, look, I do, here they are.'

'Come on then.'

And she took my hand and led me upstairs.

Are girls' bedrooms always nicer than boys' bedrooms? There was a nice white fur rug on the floor and a sort of tablecloth thing pinned to the wall with a pattern of flowers and birds on it, and there was her music-stand in the corner with sheet music on it and the violin leaning against the wardrobe. There was an Ed Sheeran calendar on the wall. But the main thing I noticed was that she had a bookcase with a really good collection of graphic novels. *Watchmen, Arkham Asylum,* the *Sandman* series – all the classics.

'Hey, I didn't know you liked this stuff.'

'Oh yeah, love it!'

'Me too!'

This was a really good thing to discover. It was a side to Claire I hadn't expected. I almost wanted to start a conversation about comic books, but it didn't seem quite the right time.

We kissed again. And pretty soon the clothes started to come off.

I'd never got this far with anyone before, except for that time with Natalie, which didn't really count. The whole thing was amazing. It made me feel like the coolest guy in the universe. And I'll tell you something else. Until then, the only bits of a woman's body I'd really been interested in were the hidden bits, the bits concealed under a bikini. But now that Claire was getting her kit off I noticed that she had beautiful knees – and beautiful shoulders – and beautiful arms – the bits you could see any day of the week were beautiful, too. Her whole body was beautiful, is what I mean I suppose, only you couldn't know that without seeing all of it.

My heart was beating like one of those things workmen use to flatten the tarmac. A piledriver, that's it, only faster. I realised I was trembling. When I took Claire in my arms, I realised she was trembling too. I kind of liked that.

So.

Anyway.

How much detail do you need here?

It happened.

We did it.

Lost our virginity together, cause Claire was one too.

It was – how can I describe it? It was cool. It made me feel, I don't know, it's hard to put into words. Sort of, like, as if I was a really little kid again. That rush of pure excitement I used to get when it was Christmas morning, or my birthday, when I was about six, and I'd run downstairs and rip open all my presents. It reminded me of that a bit. But this was better. And the funny thing was, at the same time as feeling like a really little kid, I felt like a grown-up for the first time. A man, with a man's body, doing what men do. And doing it *with* someone, being together with Claire and seeing that she was as excited as me – and she was, that face of hers couldn't lie, it had a kind of sexy expression that I'd never ever seen before but felt I somehow recognised – that was what made it so brilliant. It was cool.

Afterwards, as we lay in bed, I heard the rain drumming down on the roof and windows. It had been raining all the time, I guess, but I hadn't been listening. I'd had other things on my mind. It made a loud, insistent, complicated kind of noise, as if it was trying to tell me something. I was like, 'Hey, Claire.'

She snuggled up and gave me a little squeeze. 'Yeah?'

'Let's go and stand out in the garden. In the rain. In the nude.' I don't know why I wanted to do this. I just felt it would have been a memorable thing to do, to sort of mark the occasion. In a way, I still kind of wish we had. But we didn't.

Claire laughed. 'Oh no – it'd be much too cold. It'd be *freezing!*'

'Yeah, I spose.' I felt a bit disappointed. I had a feeling if it had been Natalie she'd have said yes to standing in the rain in the nude.

Claire snuggled up a bit more. She felt nice, so soft and warm. I put my arm round her. And then I made my big mistake.

I was like, 'I love you, Natalie.'

Immediately, she went rigid in my arms.

'What did you say?'

'Er – I said, "I love you, actually".'

'No you didn't!' said Claire. 'You said "Natalie".'

'Actually, I said "actually".'

'You said "Natalie", actually.'

She pushed me away. She was really upset.

There was only one thing to do.

'I wish you'd forget what I just said.'

A puzzled look came into her eyes. 'What are we arguing about?'

'Dunno. Come here, give us a cuddle.'

She snuggled up to me again and it was all OK. I breathed a sigh of relief. I could see I'd have to be careful here.

CHAPTER 6

So that was how Claire became my girlfriend. I felt a little bit shy about it at first. When Claire said, the next day, she was going to post our relationship status on Facebook I wasn't too sure at all about that.

'What do you want everyone to know for?'

'Why not? It's true, isn't it?'

'Yeah, but why does everyone have to know?'

'Why shouldn't they?'

'Why should they?'

Claire's face began to go into upset mode, like a little kid who's just dropped their ice cream on the pavement. 'You don't want to go out with me? Now you've got what you wanted, you're just going to walk away –'

'No, I do want to go out with you, but –'

'What, you're ashamed of me, is that it?'

'No, of course I'm not ashamed of you –'

'Then why can't I put it on Facebook?'

'Oh, all right, put it on Facebook then!'

Pretty soon the whole school knew about it, of course. I could see people looking at me and Claire, and overheard snatches of conversation, 'Have you heard the news? Adam's going out with Claire!' 'What, Claire *Brown*?'. Martin came up to me at break, grinning all over his face, and he was like, 'Adam and Claire, sitting in a tree, Kay Eye Ess Ess Eye En Gee!'

I was like, 'Oh shut up, Martin. What are you, like eight years old?'

Dirk was like, 'I thought you wanted to go out with Natalie, though?'

'Yeah, well… life is full of surprises, innit?'

Dirk took a breath as if he was about to speak, but then he didn't say anything. I didn't quite like the way he started to look so thoughtful.

My instinct was to not hang around with Claire too much at school, but this was difficult because we were in the same English class. Also, she did want to hang around with me. After our lesson on *Measure for Measure* she waited for me at the door and we went off to the hall for lunch together, and as we were going down the corridor she slipped her hand into mine.

At just that moment Mervyn Stott came by with his mate Kai Howlett. They nudged each other and Stott said something I didn't quite catch, and they laughed. I looked at Claire and she'd obviously heard it. Her face looked red and shocked as if someone had just slapped her.

I let go of her hand and moved a bit closer to Stotty. 'What did you say?'

'Nothing.' Stott edged away. I had a bit of a reputation after the fight with Renwick, of course, and I was about five inches taller than him.

'I think you did say something. I wish you'd tell me what it was.'

Claire pulled at my arm. 'Don't bother, Adam, he's not worth it.'

Stott spoke unwillingly, like the words were being pulled out of his mouth by a dentist. 'I said… Taking… your heifer… out to graze… are you?'

'It was just a joke,' Kai said.

'Yeah? Well, here's another joke. Look into my eyes. Look deep into my eyes. I wish you two would get down on all-fours and walk out to the school field and eat a mouthful of grass each, OK?'

They immediately dropped down on all-fours and moseyed on down the corridor with their arses stuck up in the air, and out through the glass double-doors at the end onto the field. We saw them in the distance with their heads down, going at the grass.

Claire had her astonished face on. 'How – how –?'

'Oh, I took one of those hypnotism courses. I knew it would come in handy one day.'

'That's amazing!' Claire took my hand again. 'Adam…'

'Yeah?'

'Am I a heifer?'

'No, don't be silly! You're more of a… gazelle.'

'A fat gazelle? A pregnant gazelle?'

'No, a normal gazelle.'

And we went into lunch. But I noticed Claire only had a salad.

So me and Claire were an item. And we had a lot of fun over the next few months. In my experience, people talking about what a wonderful time they've had gets really boring and annoying after a while, so I'm going to skate over the next three months a bit. Here's a list of some of the highlights:

- Took Claire to an Ed Sheeran concert at the Hammersmith Apollo. We had front-row seats, of course, and afterwards we went backstage and met Ed and the band. He was really nice. We all ate fried chicken (I wished for a bucket of it) and Claire borrowed a violin and played along with Ed singing 'Galway Girl'. And we all became friends on Facebook and promised to stay in touch.
- Went to New York for the weekend with Claire. Stayed in the Waldorf Astoria. Had lots of sex.
- Went to Paris for the weekend. Stayed in the George V. Impressed Claire with my perfect French, which I'd wished for. Had lots of sex.
- Took Claire for a weekend in Devon and we went swimming in the sea. I love the sea. I reckon in a previous life I was a mackerel or something (if I believed in reincarnation, which I don't). Claire turned out to be a brilliant swimmer. Better than me, in fact.
- Wished I could swim as well as Claire.
- Took Claire scuba-diving off the Great Barrier Reef.
- Ate out in posh restaurants whenever we felt like it.

This last one caused me what you might term a moral dilemma. I knew that Claire was worried about being overweight. In fact she had a bit of an obsession about it. She'd ask me if she looked fat about once a day. I always said no but it didn't stop her asking the same question the very next day. And whenever we went to a restaurant I could see her worrying about how many calories she was consuming. At the same time, she loved her food and found it hard to resist the desserts. I could of course have simply wished she'd lose a few pounds and that would have made her happy. But I didn't want to get into the whole area of designing someone else's body to a given set of specifications. That would have just seemed a bit too mad. So in the end I simply wished that neither of us would get any fatter, no matter how many times we ate out. I thought that was a reasonable compromise.

Of course I didn't just use my wishes on me and Claire. I used them to improve what you might call the texture of life generally. For instance:

- Every morning, if I didn't feel like getting up, I wished it was an hour earlier.
- When I did feel like getting up, I wished that I was washed and dressed in the twinkling of an eye.
- Wished there was a thousand pounds in my trouser pocket every day.
- Astounded Yvonne by playing 'Flight of the Bumble Bee' on the piano in under a minute.
- Joined the chess club at school and beat the pants off Mr Tubby.

I carried on playing football for the school team, of course, banging in spectacular goals – acrobatic volleys, flying headers, scorpion kicks, all that. But I wasn't a totally selfish player. I set up chances for other people too, especially Martin. I made nearly as many assists as I scored goals. All the same, I was the team's top scorer and thanks to me we put together a run of twelve wins on the spin.

Martin was like, 'I dunno what's happened to you! You just became the most amazing player overnight!'

'Late developer, I guess.'

'Yeah, but you didn't *develop*, it was like a kinda miraculous trans-formation! You could turn pro if you keep this up, I mean it.'

I was like, 'No, no.' Modest, you know. 'I thought you were the one who was gonna turn pro.'

Martin pulled a face. A grimace. 'Look, I've been playing every week for the school and for Woodford Wanderers for years, and I still haven't been spotted. If I was gonna get picked up by a talent scout it woulda happened by now.'

'You never know. You could be playing first-team football for Arsenal by the start of next season!'

'Yeah, right.'

'I wish that would happen, though. I wish you'd play for Arsenal next season.'

'Yeah, well, *wishing* doesn't change anything, does it?'

I turned away to hide a smile. 'You never know,' I said again.

I felt pleased with myself, like I'd bought him a special secret birthday present or organised a surprise party.

I did a lot of cool stuff with Emily, too. Like, she's got all these pic-ture books, you know the sort of thing, ones about the North Pole with smiling polar bears and ones about the African savannah with smiling lions, etc., etc. So sometimes I'd be reading one of these with her and I'd go, 'Hey, Emily – wanna go to the jungle?'

'Yes, pease.'

'OK – I wish we were in the jungle.'

And there we'd be, standing in the undergrowth under these great tall trees, all hot and humid, listening to the screeches of the mon-keys and the parrots.

Or another time I'd go, 'Hey, Emily – wanna go to the desert?'

'Yes, pease.'

And there we were standing on top of a sand dune, watching a camel train file past.

We went to the North Pole, too, but we didn't hang about there, I can tell you. It was bloody freezing. It was so cold it made Emily cry, and I had to take her to the Bahamas for the afternoon to cheer her up.

She told Mum and Dad about these adventures and they just laughed and said what a fantastic imagination she had. I hadn't told Mum and Dad about my wishes. It was none of their business. I made a wish that they'd just accept any weird stuff I did, without scratching their heads over it.

I didn't tell Claire about my wishes either. I liked the fact that I hadn't had to wish for Claire to be my girlfriend, she just thought I was gorgeous of her own accord. So I wanted to keep her separate from the wishing thing. I mean, she benefited from it, but she didn't have to know about it. Obviously, she asked about how I'd got all this money and stuff. I told her it was from being an internet millionaire. When the questions got too difficult to answer I just wished she'd forget about it, and that was that. This was a really convenient thing to be able to do, by the way. It made for a pretty smooth relationship. We never had rows.

The only fly in the ointment was, I did still pine for Natalie a bit. I mean, I was happy with Claire, don't get me wrong. But I still felt I'd have been happier with Natalie. Every time I saw her at school I got that feeling I said about before, like being jabbed in the heart with a pin. And what with her being Claire's best friend, I saw quite a bit of her. To tell the truth, I hadn't completely given up on her. I thought that Claire was like a temporary girlfriend (even though I did like her, don't get me wrong) – but I felt Natalie was really the one for me, the one I was born for. It was true that she didn't quite seem to agree, but she'd get it in the end. I was always trying to impress her, making jokes and stuff, trying to catch her eye. Claire noticed this now and again and didn't like it. Not that I could blame her.

She was like, 'You're always staring at Natalie. When she's around, you don't look at anyone else. You don't look at me at all.'

'What are you on about? I'm always looking at you.'

'You're not! You prefer Natalie, it's completely obvious. Why don't you ask her out instead?'

'She doesn't wanna go out with me.'

'Oh, so you would go out with her if she wanted to, would you?'

She was getting really upset, tears trembling on the brink of her eye-lids. So I was like, 'I wish we could just forget this conversation.'

And that was that.

Like I said, it was pretty convenient.

The only one who knew about my wishes was Dirk. I kept my word and didn't fix any more Orient games. They eventually pulled out of trouble by themselves and didn't get relegated. But it was close. They had to win the last match of the season to save themselves, and they did, 1–0 against Dagenham and Redbridge.

Dirk was like, 'See?' as we drove away from the ground in my open-topped Jeep (oh yeah, I forgot to say I wished for that as well. It was done in an orange and green camouflage pattern, pretty funky). 'It was more exciting leaving them to get out of it them-selves, wasn't it?'

'You wouldn't say that if they'd lost today.'

'That's the risk you run. That's what life's all about.'

'Yeah, right.'

'Honest, Adam. I reckon you'd be better off without your wishes. Why don't you wish not to have them any more?'

'Yeah, right. Like that's gonna happen. Listen – you've been get-ting into the O's for nothing all season, cause I wished for season tickets, right? And you've got about ten grand and a brand new computer that I've wished for you, right? And I've taken you flying. You don't mind getting the benefits, do you? So don't start lecturing me.'

This was all true, what I'd just said. Dirk had asked me for money a few times, as well as a new computer, and we'd been night-flying on a number of occasions. He looked a bit lost for words now I'd reminded him of it. I felt kind of pleased with myself, cause it wasn't often I got the better of him in an argument.

I was like, 'I reckon you're just jealous, cause I can do anything I want. But look, I've told you, I'll wish for stuff for you too, more stuff, anything you want. I'll make you Prime Minister, if you like.'

Dirk's like, 'No thanks.' He goes kind of pensive. Then he's like, 'I'm not jealous. But I have to admit – it makes me uneasy, you having all these wishes. I wish you didn't have them. It's – it's too much power. It's frightening.'

'Don't worry, I won't do anything crazy. Hey, look, how about I wish you didn't feel uneasy any more?'

'No way, man!' goes Dirk. He's kind of sharp about it. 'Don't start wishing stuff about me. You just let me be myself, OK?'

'OK, OK.'

I couldn't blame him for feeling uneasy about it. Infinite wishes. I mean, wow. It can't be all that comfortable, being friends with someone who's got the powers of a god. If it had been Dirk, not me, with the infinite number of wishes, I wonder how I'd have felt?

CHAPTER 7

June came, and so did the AS levels. Without my wishes, I'd have been shitting bricks, of course, but now all I had to do was wish for four A-star grades and worry no more. I asked Dirk if he wanted some help, too.

'Get you any grades you want, mate. Just say the word.'

Dirk's like, 'No thanks.'

'Why not? Save you a lot of hassle.'

'You just don't get it, do you?'

I hate it when people say that. I reckon that phrase should be banned by law. It's so frustrating. Patronising.

I was like, 'Suit yourself.'

'Don't mess with my grades, right?'

'OK, OK.'

I felt a bit frustrated with him. I was only trying to help, you know? I knew he'd do OK on his own anyway, but there was no need to be so arsy about it.

Claire was dead worried about the exams. She was pretty bright and didn't really have much to worry about. She'd got a decent set of GCSEs after all, and the subjects she was doing now were her hand-picked favourites. But she kept having this fantasy that it would all go belly-shaped on the day.

I was like, 'Don't you mean belly-up? Or pear-shaped?'

'You see, I can't even get the expression right! What's gonna happen to me in the exams?'

She was worried that her mind would just go blank. The ironic thing was I'd already wished that she wouldn't fail any, but I couldn't tell her that. She kept phoning me to talk about it. I'd be like, 'I wish you'd stop worrying,' and that would work, but the wish only seemed to last a day. The next day she'd phone up again and we'd have to have the exact same conversation all over again. It was a bit wearing, as my mum would say.

The truth is... I feel bad saying it, but I was getting a bit fed up going out with Claire. I mean, we'd had a good three months together. We'd done some highly enjoyable stuff. Only – well, she seemed to like me more than I was comfortable with. I don't know why, it sort of got on my nerves, the way she needed me so much.

Plus I couldn't help thinking, considering I had an infinite number of wishes, that I could do better for myself. There were so many babes out there. Like Claire's friend Shushmita, for instance. She was proper fanciable. She'd started singing in this band with some other Indian kids. They were called Kiss My Chuddies. And – obviously – there was Natalie. I still couldn't quite bring myself to believe I had no chance there. Even though I'd heard it from her own lips when I was a fly.

But I wasn't ready to dump Claire just yet. I wanted to get something started with someone else first – preferably Natalie (without using a wish, of course – that was still the rule). Plus, it wouldn't have been fair to dump poor old Claire just before the exams, the state she was in. I could have just dumped her and wished she wouldn't mind, I know. But then, *I* wouldn't have liked that. It would have been kind of insulting to me. People might even think I was the one who got dumped, if Claire obviously didn't give a toss about being without me.

So I put off doing anything till after the exams. Till after the party, in fact. Because, yeah, I'd decided to have a party. I was going to hold a great big post-exam bash at my house. It was going to be the mother of all parties.

It was going to be the mother of all parties.

I looked round the house and I just thought, *Wow*. I'd enlarged it specially for the occasion. When you came in the hall, you saw this great big marble floor, with black and white squares like a chessboard. There was a fountain playing at the end. There was a massive crystal chandelier hanging from the ceiling and a flock of little multi-coloured birds fluttering around underneath it (I don't know what sort they were, I just wished for some red and yellow and green and blue birds to come along and do the honours). Then a great big sweeping staircase leading up to this gallery with rooms all along it, and then the staircase went sweeping up to another gallery just like it with more rooms, and then up to another gallery above that. So no shortage of rooms for people to cop off in. Every room had a double four-poster bed with silk sheets, and an en suite bathroom and toilet. In my experience, there's never enough toilets at parties.

Another thing about parties is, the drink tends to run out. Well, it wasn't going to run out at mine. In the kitchen there were tables and tables with bottles and bottles of wine and beer and vodka and whisky and Bacardi Breezers, plus coke and lemonade and orange juice and all that stuff. There was food, too. People don't normally eat the food at parties. They just stub fag ends out in it, or drop it on the floor and tread it into the carpet. But they'd eat the food at mine. There was Burger King and Subway, plus pizzas and Chinese and Indian takeaways. And it was all free.

Then there was the garden. I'd made it ten times as big as before and it was all floodlit. There was this bit with chairs and tables, and there was this little wood with lanterns hanging from the trees, and there was a heated swimming pool that had a little island in the middle with a palm tree sticking out of it.

I looked round it all and I thought it looked pretty good. Then I sat down in the hall next to the fountain, with a glass of champagne. It was only eight o'clock and no one had arrived yet. I'd sent Mum and Dad and Emily off to spend the night at a bed and breakfast in Devon – we used to stay there when I was a kid, before Emily was born, and I thought it would be nice for them to go back there and show it to Emily. So I sat on my own and listened to the fountain tinkling away and watched the birds fluttering around. I was expecting to feel really happy, but then this kind of funny mood came over me. It was a bit frustrating.

All this stuff I'd wished for suddenly seemed really, like, precarious. As if I'd ordered it on credit and it could get carted back to the shop if I didn't keep up the payments. I knew with just one wish I could make it all disappear. It was like it was all *unreal*, like a dream. And I just thought, 'What's the point?'

I started to feel kind of sorry for myself. I knew I had no reason to feel sorry for myself, right. But I just couldn't help it. Maybe it was post-exam blues. But that was a joke, wasn't it? Cause I hadn't really done the exams, not really *done* them, I mean they hadn't involved any work or stress. So why did I feel so down? I don't know, but I did. I started to feel pretty lonely, sitting there by the fountain with those stupid birds twittering and fluttering about.

Bobbligrubs came shambling up and shoved his wet nose into my hand. I looked into his doggy brown eyes. I was like, 'What's the point of it all, Bobbligrubs?'

He didn't answer, of course. And I wasn't about to wish that he could talk again. I didn't want any more of that stuff about what he'd like to do with the horny bitch at number 19.

I was glad when the doorbell rang. That'd be Dirk. I'd asked him to come round early.

Dirk was like, 'Wow, man!' He was turning round and round like he was lost or something, looking at the fountain and the birds and the galleries. 'This is incredible!'

'Glad you like it.'

'I didn't say I liked it, I just said it was incredible.'

'Have a drink. Have some champagne.'

'I'll just have a Dr Pepper, thanks. I wanna keep a clear head tonight.'

'Why's that, then?'

'Cause… I'm hoping to get lucky,' goes Dirk, looking a bit self-conscious.

'Are you?' I pricked up my ears a bit. Dirk's never had a girlfriend as far as I know. I guess we were both pretty late starters. He must think about that stuff. But he doesn't talk about it much. Perhaps he thinks it wouldn't be cool.

'Yeah, I am. I hope.'

'Got anyone particular in mind?'

'Yeah.'

'Who is it, then?'

'Just someone.'

'Who?'

'Someone nice.'

'Go on, Dirk, tell us. Who is it?'

He gave a sneaky kind of smirk. I'd never known Dirk act quite like this. 'Wait and see.'

'Go on, don't be annoying. Tell us. Or I'll just wish I knew.'

'OK, OK, look. You're going out with Claire, now, right?'

'You know I am.'

'Well, so that means Natalie's, like, free, then, doesn't it?'

I got this kind of sickening feeling. Dirk was on a loser – my wish would see to that. But how was it going to work? If they both wanted to go out with each other, what was going to stop them? I might have created a pretty tricky situation. Whatever happened, anyway, Dirk was going to be disappointed. I felt bad about it, I really did. I decided it was better to just sidestep the whole thing.

I was like, 'I wish it's not Natalie you wanna go out with.'

'No, it's not Natalie,' goes Dirk immediately.

'Who is it, then?'

Dirk opens his mouth and then closes it again. Like he's baffled, cause he had been about to say Natalie and now he doesn't know what name to say. He's like, 'It's someone, I do know that.' I can see him thinking. 'I know,' he goes after a bit. 'It's Shushmita.'

'Oh, Shushmita. Right.'

I could see how he'd got there. Natalie, Claire and Shushmita all went round together and you tended to think of them together. Natalie was out, Claire was spoken for, so that only left Shushmita. But to tell the truth, I was completely and utterly sickened and pissed off about it. I fancied Shushmita myself and I knew it would make me jealous to see Dirk and her together.

'She's great, isn't she?' goes Dirk.

'Yeah, very nice.'

'She's a great singer, don't you think?'

'Yeah, very good.'

For a second or two, I even wondered if I should wish that she wouldn't fancy him. That would piss on his firework. I didn't, though. I could have done, but I didn't. That was pretty good of me, wasn't it? What you might call heroic restraint. But I reckon it was the strain of resisting this temptation that made me do what I did later in the evening...

But I'm running ahead of myself. We'll get to that bit soon enough.

People started turning up about half nine. I'd invited everyone from Years 12 and 13, even people I didn't like. Such as Steve Renwick and his pathetic mates Mervyn Stott, Ethan Crump and Kai Howlett. It was kind of fun to watch their jaws drop when they got inside. Outside it still looked like an ordinary terraced house, you see, but like the Tardis it was bigger inside than out. You came through the front door and it was like being in Buckingham Palace or some-where.

Martin turned up and practically danced his way into the house. 'Guess what, guess what?' He was so happy he was almost singing.

'What's up?'

'I've been asked to trial for Arsenal!'

'Get outta here!'

'No, after the game today a scout came up and took all my details, they want me to try out for the youth team!'

'Sweet.'

'Now I just gotta hope I don't screw up the trial.'

'You won't. I guarantee it.'

'It's so amazing, it just came out of the blue, just when I'd given up hope!'

'Let me get you a drink to celebrate.'

'Just a fizzy water, I really have to take care of myself now…'

My mood lifted a bit. Nice to see the old wishes working away there. I'd known Martin since we were about five, so it felt somehow like I'd done a favour to his younger self, shaping a golden future for that football-mad little kid he used to be.

So that was OK, but then my mood got more complicated as more guests streamed in. Natalie and Claire came along with Shush-mita and the other members of Kiss My Chuddies. Shushmita looked really pleased to see Dirk, which annoyed me. They went off into a corner together and started talking really intensely. I don't know what they were talking about. Philosophy or some crap like that, probably. Dirk had this really, like, earnest expression on and Shushmita was looking up at him with her great dark eyes like he was some sort of guru. It was pretty sickening.

Claire was like, 'Hello, Adam.' A little bit reproachful, like I should be taking more notice of her. It annoyed me a bit, so I just said 'Hi, Claire', casual-like, and gave her a kiss on the cheek. Then I turned my attention to Natalie.

'What do you think of the place?'

'It's amazing! Where did you get those birds?'

'Oh, they just, er, flew in through the window. Can I get you a drink?'

'I'll have a white wine spritzer, please.'

Claire was like, in a loud, emphatic kind of voice, 'And so will I!'

As I was walking away, I heard Claire go 'See?' Not sure what she meant.

When I came back with the drinks, they were talking about the exams.

I was like, 'How do you reckon you did?'

Natalie was like, 'All right, I hope. But you can't really tell for sure, can you?'

'I can tell for sure. I'm gonna get four A-stars, I am.'

'You're very arrogant, aren't you?' goes Claire. She said it with a sort of nasty nip in her voice, if you know what I mean. I couldn't have been more shocked if Bobbligrubs had turned round and bitten me.

I was like, 'What's the matter with you?'

'I'll leave you two lovebirds alone together,' goes Natalie. I watched her beautiful round bum as she walked away. I felt like moaning aloud.

Claire was like, 'Look, why are you giving me the hard shoulder?'

'It's not the hard shoulder, it's the cold shoulder.'

'Well, whatever sort of shoulder it is, you're giving it to me!' said Claire in a wobbly voice. And then she started to cry.

Out of the corner of my eye, I saw Dirk and Shushmita still huddled together in earnest conversation. I swear she was stroking his arm. A pang of jealousy shot through me like toothache.

'You're not even taking notice of me now!' goes Claire in a wailing kind of way. Tears were spilling down her cheeks and her face had gone all red.

'I wish you'd stop crying!' That did the trick. But she still looked miserable, with the corners of her mouth turned down. 'Look, I wish you'd cheer up. Tell you what, I wish you'd go and get me some noodles from the Chinese takeaway over there. Get some for yourself too.'

She perked up a bit and cheerfully trotted off to the Chinese takeaway. There was already a queue there, so I'd bought myself a bit of time. I set off to look for Natalie.

I'd made a desperate decision.

On the way, I bumped into Steve Renwick. Literally bumped into him, cause I was in such a hurry.

'Watch it, Gowers.'

'Or what?'

Renwick fixed his icy blue stare on me. 'You done me once. I ain't complaining. But you might not get so lucky the next time.'

'Yeah, right.'

'And there will be a next time. You can bet on that.'

'Thanks for the tip.'

'Next time, I'll smash your face in.'

'Yeah, like, I'm shitting myself.'

Typical Renwick, of course. Anyone else would have steered well clear of someone who'd beaten the crap out of them like I'd beaten the crap out of him. But Renwick's a nutter. He's got to try and get his own back, it's part of his insane warrior's code. I could have sorted him out there and then, of course, but I couldn't be bothered. I had more urgent things to do. I tried to step past him. He grabbed me by the shoulder.

He was like, 'What about right now? Out in the garden? Come on, if you think you're hard enough.'

'Get off. Look, I wish you'd remain rooted to the spot for five minutes.'

I moved away and he tried to follow, but his feet wouldn't budge. It was like they were glued to the floor. He started shouting 'Me legs! I can't move me legs!' Mervyn and a couple of his other followers came over and started trying to get his feet to shift, but with no success, obviously.

I sort of smirked to myself and went on looking for Natalie. It was pretty crowded by now and I couldn't see her anywhere. Then I had an idea. I didn't need to look for her, did I? I had my wishes. I'd never need to look for anyone or anything ever again. So I was like, 'I wish I was wherever Natalie is.'

The next instant, I was standing in a very small room.

And Natalie was sitting on the toilet in front of me.

She literally jumped clear off the seat when she saw me. Her eyes went as wide and round as saucers.

I decided to try and cool it out.

'Hi, Natalie. Just popped in to see if, er, you're all right for toilet paper.'

Natalie's mouth opened. I knew she was going to scream. I'd seen Emily do a similar expression before screaming.

'Right, well, I see you're OK for loo roll, so I'll, well, I'll be off then.'

I opened the door, went out onto the landing and closed it behind me. Then the screams began. It was a terrible noise. I didn't know Natalie could scream like that. It sounded like a pig getting its throat cut. Not that I've ever heard a pig getting its throat cut. But I imagine that's what it would sound like. People started running up the stairs to see what was the matter.

I was like, 'Natalie, I wish you'd stop screaming.' The screaming stopped, like someone had just turned the radio off. Then I was like, 'I wish you lot would all go back downstairs,' and all the busybodies and nosey parkers who were running up the stairs turned round and trooped back down again. Then I turned and spoke through the toilet door. 'Listen, Natalie, I wish you'd forget that I was in the toilet just now. OK? Just forget it.'

'OK,' came Natalie's voice through the toilet door.

After a bit I heard the toilet flush and the door opened. Natalie came out looking really confused.

I was like, 'Natalie! What's the matter?' in this really sympathetic voice.

'I don't know – I have the feeling that something weird just happened to me – it gave me a terrible shock.' She passed her hand across her forehead, just like actors do on the telly.

'What was it? What happened?'

'I don't know. I can't remember.'

'Well, I wish you felt better about it.'

'Yes, I do feel better now,' goes Natalie. She smiles. 'Thanks, Adam.'

'What for?'

'For being so sympathetic.'

'Oh, you know. That's just the kind of guy I am.'

'You must think I'm a weirdo.'

'Not really. I mean, not at all. Listen, I've been meaning to talk to you.'

'Have you? What about?'

'Well, about – you know – you and me.'

'How do you mean?'

'You know. Maybe we should go out together. You and me. As an item, you know?'

'But what about Claire?'

'But Claire's been going out with me for three months now! It's time I gave someone else a turn, don't you reckon? With a body like mine, it's only fair to share it around!'

This was supposed to be a joke, obviously. But I'd noticed before that Natalie didn't tend to laugh at my jokes. She certainly didn't laugh at this one. She looked at me like I'd just farted.

'I don't think we should talk about this any more. You should think about Claire. She really likes you.'

I gave a big, deep sigh. I really had tried, hadn't I? I mean I really had. I'd tried doing it the proper way. And she'd turned me down.

So there was nothing for it now but the improper way.

'I wish you were madly in love with me, Natalie.'

'Oh, but I am!' She grabbed my hand and started kissing it. 'I am in love with you! You mean more to me than the sun and the moon and the stars!'

I was like, 'Blimey.'

'You're amazing! You're tops! You're the cream of the crop!'

'So – will you go to bed with me, then?'

Her eyes lit up like the eyes of a Hallowe'en pumpkin. She gave a wicked little smile. 'Just watch me!'

She grabbed me by the hand, flung open the nearest bedroom door and pulled me in.

We both kind of dived and fell onto the bed and started pulling each other's clothes off. Pretty soon, we were both down to our underwear. She was wearing this kind of red lacy stuff with little flowers on it. Very pretty. Her party underwear, I suppose. And the sight of it drove me wild. I don't quite know how to explain it – it was like every little cell in my body was coming to life, waking up and stretching. I'd been in this position before, of course. But that time I'd bottled out. Or done the decent thing, depending how you look at it. This time I wasn't going to do the decent thing. I was going to do the indecent thing. And nothing was going to stop me.

Yeah, right.

The door burst open and there stood Claire holding a bowl of noodles.

'I've been looking for you all over the –' she began, then stopped. 'What's this? What's going on? Why have you taken all your clothes off?'

We hadn't even got them all off yet, that was the frustrating thing.

I thought I'd better end this scene pretty damn quickly, so I was like, 'I wish –'

But that was as far as I got, cause the next second a flying bowl of noodles hit me straight in the face.

I was like, 'Ow!' cause they were pretty hot. I started wiping bits of noodle and spring onions and prawns and soy sauce off my face. Meanwhile, Claire started on Natalie. Her face expressed pure rage. She looked like an emoji of anger.

'How could you do this to me?'

Natalie was like, 'I love him. I can't help that. I love him and I've got to have him!'

'Well, you can't have him! He's mine!'

'Not any more. It's me he wants! That's why he's in this bedroom with me in his underpants! Which I was just about to remove when you came barging in!'

'You bitch!' screamed Claire. I'd never heard her talk like that before.

Then she jumped on Natalie and started hitting her. And Natalie started hitting her back. They bounced around on the bed, kicking and punching and pulling each other's hair. It was mad. They were both really going for it. I don't know who'd have won in the end. If I'd had to put a bet on it, I'd probably have gone for Claire, with her weight advantage. But of course, I didn't let things get that far.

I was like, 'I wish these noodles were off my face.'

Then I was like, 'I wish you two would stop fighting.'

They stopped and stared at each other, panting for breath. I didn't know what to do next. I kind of felt it was time I was out of there.

I was like, 'I wish I was in the garden.'

It was peaceful out in the garden. Tranquil. I stood under the trees in the lantern-light, trying to collect my thoughts. I took some deep breaths. I started to calm down.

Then I felt a tap on my shoulder.

'Hey, Gowers.'

'What?'

I turned round to see Steve Renwick's fist travelling towards my face at the speed of sound.

'I wish –'

But that was as far as I got, because the next second Renwick's fist sort of exploded in my face. I saw this single bright star inside my head and it broke up into lots of smaller ones. The star did, I mean, not my head. It was like watching a firework. I fell flat on my back.

And then Renwick started kicking me.

You can hardly blame me if I felt a bit pissed off at this point. I mean, it was my party and I was having a completely crap time. So far, I'd watched Dirk copping off with Shushmita, I'd had a row with Claire, I'd failed once again to hook up with Natalie, I'd got a bowl of hot noodles chucked in my face, I'd been smashed on the nose and now I was having the shit kicked out of me in the garden by Renwick. I mean, as parties go it's not what you'd call a brilliant success, is it?

So I started to get a bit angry. In other words, I completely lost it. I was like, 'I wish I was as strong as a gorilla.'

Then I jumped up and started giving Renwick a going-over.

I hadn't really realised quite how strong gorillas are. They certainly are extraordinarily strong. All I did was shake Renwick a bit. And squeeze him a bit. And chuck him around a bit. And bash him about a bit.

I suppose I did let myself go a bit, really, come to think of it.

Anyway, it was too much for Renwick. After a couple of minutes of this treatment, he gave up the struggle and fell down dead.

Completely dead.

Dead as a post, as Claire might say.

That was the end of the party, really. I just didn't feel like it after that.

I wished Renwick was alive again, of course. I sent him home in a taxi. He looked kind of dazed. I wished Claire and Natalie would forget what had happened up in the bedroom. I sent them home, too. And everyone else. They all went off into the night, saying, 'Great party Adam!' Yeah, right. Dirk had his arm round Shushmita. He looked pretty pleased with himself, like a dog with a bone. A bloody great big bone, a dinosaur's thighbone or something.

'Good night, Adam! Great party!'

'Yeah, good night.'

After they'd all gone, I wished away the lanterns and the fountain and the Burger King and the Chinese and Indian takeaways and the marble floor and the sweeping staircase and the stupid multi-coloured birds, the lot. I wished it was all gone and the house was back to normal. Like I hadn't kept up the repayment instalments and it had all been repossessed.

The house seemed strangely small and gloomy after that. But it suited my mood.

I went up to bed.

There didn't seem much else to do.

CHAPTER 8

'It's fantastic, isn't it?'

'What is?'

I knew exactly what Dirk was talking about. But it annoyed me, so I pretended I didn't.

'You know.'

'No, I don't.'

'Yes you do.'

'Oh, all right, then, I do.'

'And it is fantastic, isn't it?'

'Yeah, fantastic.'

We were sitting out in Dirk's back garden, drinking Dr Peppers. I could tell by the sickening dreamy look in Dirk's eyes he was thinking about what he got up to with Shushmita.

'I never knew how good life could be till I met Shushmita.'

'What are you chatting about? You met her years ago.'

'No, I mean till I started going out with her. Or staying in with her!'

'Yeah, well, good for you.'

'You must feel the same about Claire, I spose.'

'Er, yeah. That's right, I do.'

I was still with Claire. Being as Natalie wouldn't have anything to do with me unless she was in a wish-induced trance, and being as Shushmita was spoken for by Mr Smugface here, I'd reckoned I might as well stay with Claire for now. Since the party I'd been quite a bit nicer to her. In fact, I found that the relationship, as Claire liked to call it, went a lot better when I was being nice. As long as I could remember to keep it up.

'You know what Freud said?'

'I spect he said a lot of things. He probably said, "Where are my keys?" and, "I'm just popping down to the shops." And, "Those doughnuts look nice." And, –'

'OK, OK, but one particular thing he said was, "The only things that can save you are work and love." What do you think of that?'

'I dunno. I dunno what it means. What's he on about, "save" you?'

'It means the only things that make life worth living, that make you able to put up with all the crap, right, is being in love or working.'

'So?'

'Well, I dunno about working, but as far as being in love goes, he was dead right.'

'Oh, you're in love, are you?'

He gave this kind of sheepish smile. Well, it was more of a randy ram's smile. 'Yeah, I think I am.'

'Well, I'm really happy for you.'

'What's the matter? Are you being sarcastic?'

I was like, 'No, no, I mean it, I really am happy for you. Really.'

I didn't mean it, obviously, but I didn't want him thinking I was jealous. Even though I was. I didn't begrudge Dirk a moderate amount of happiness. I *wanted* him to be happy.

I just didn't want him to be more happy than me.

I got up. 'Anyway, look, I gotta go now.'

'Where you going?'

'Gonna see a man about a job.'

'What job?' goes Dirk.

'Wait and see.' I made a wish, and I was gone.

You see, Dirk had got me thinking with this thing that Freud said. Not about the love thing. I'd decided to let the love thing sit for a while. But about work. Maybe I felt sort of restless and discontented cause I wasn't doing anything useful. Maybe a job was what I needed. Cause there wasn't much point staying on for Year 13 really, was there? I could have as many A-levels as I liked just by wishing for them, if I wanted, which I didn't, particularly.

So, what job should I get? Well, if you could have any job in the world, whatever you wanted, what would you choose? Professional footballer, right? I suppose you might have said film star or pop star, but footballer has got to be pretty high on anyone's list. Just think of it. Running out onto the pitch every Saturday – tens of thousands of people cheering you – the goals, the glory, the hero-worship…

I'd already bestowed all this on Martin as a gift. So why shouldn't I bestow it on myself too?

My wish took me straight to the office of Barry Blodger, the Orient manager. He was sitting behind a desk wearing a tracksuit. Barry was wearing it, I mean, not the desk. He was a middle-aged bloke with a red face and lots of gold rings on his stubby fingers. All round the office, on shelves and in a glass display cabinet, there were silver cups and trophies. I don't know what they were for. As far as I knew the O's had never won anything. Not a sausage. Maybe he'd bought them as a job lot in a car boot sale. Just to brighten up the office a bit.

You might be wondering why I chose Orient, when I could have joined Martin at Arsenal, or walked into Man United or Man City. Or Bayern Munich or Real Madrid or Barcelona. But it didn't really matter who I played for. Any team would be unbeatable with me in the line-up. And I liked the idea of helping my local team. Barry Blodger didn't know it yet, but I was going to put Orient on the map of world football.

He looked up at me questioningly.

'Yes, mate, what can I do you for?'

I'm like, 'I'm here about the job.'

'You what? What job?'

'I heard you had a vacancy for a striker.'

'Sorry, son, who are you?'

'Adam Gowers is my name. Being a striker is my game.'

'You want a trial, you mean.'

'Yeah, all right, then.'

'How old are you?'

'17.'

Barry Blodger looked taken aback. 'You look older than that. Who do you play for?'

'No one. Just my school team.'

Barry Blodger puffed out his cheeks. 'Hmm. Normally people

come to us through the scouting system, you see. But if no one's ever seen you play…'

'Trust me, you want me in your team.'

'You see, if we gave a trial to everyone who turned up wanting one…'

'I'm not talking about everyone. Just me.'

'Well, you just give me one good reason why I should.'

'OK.'

To describe what I did next, I need to explain that a) there was a window behind Barry Blodger's desk, b) the window was open, c) it looked out onto the pitch and d) you could only see the middle of the pitch, not the goals at either end. There was a football on top of a cabinet. I took it and placed it on the floor. I muttered my wish under my breath.

Then I booted the ball as hard as I could.

'Hey, what the –'

Barry Blodger ducked as the ball zoomed over his head. It whizzed through the window, took a sharp right turn and passed out of sight.

'You bloody idiot, what do you think –'

'Just look out the window, Barry.'

Barry Blodger got up and stuck his head out the window. Then he turned back to me with a look of amazement on his face.

So that was how I got the job at Orient.

After all, there can't be many strikers who can bend the ball in a right angle and put it in the back of the net from 200 metres away.

When they can't even see the goal.

'Hey, Mum, I've got a job.'

'A job?' Mum put down her cup of camomile tea and looked at me in surprise. She was drinking camomile tea because I'd wished that she and Dad would stop drinking alcohol all the time. They both looked a lot healthier for it. And there weren't any more complaints from Dad's clients. So that was all right. But it didn't make them get on much better, really. They were still pretty grumpy. They didn't have so many rows cause they didn't let themselves go so much.

But you could tell that, under the surface, they weren't exactly crazy about each other.

'Wassa job?' goes Emily.

'It's work you do to get money.'

'Wass money?'

'It's stuff you buy stuff with.'

'Wass stuff?'

I had to pass on that one.

'What's the job?' goes my mum.

'I'm gonna be a footballer. With the O's.'

'You're not!'

'I am. Look, here's the contract.'

My dad put his newspaper down. He seemed really delighted. Beaming all over his face. 'Good for you, Adam. You must have inherited a footballing gene from me.'

'From you?' goes my mum, in a tone of what you might call extreme scepticism.

'Oh, yes. I used to be pretty nifty at football when I was younger.'

He paused, and in my head I'm going like, three, two, one…

'I played for the county, you know,' goes Dad, bang on cue.

There was a deafening roar as I led the team out on the pitch. And this time, I'm not kidding. There really was a deafening roar, cause I'd wished for one. The sky was blue, the grass was green, my Orient strip was red and white. As we warmed up, I entertained the capacity crowd with my dazzling ball skills, juggling the ball with my feet, my knees, my head. This brought more cheers from the crowd. Every eye was on me because my photo was in the programme, and the chairman had written a piece saying I was going to be the best player since Pele. In fact he was underplaying it a bit. I'd wished to be as good as Pele, George Best, Johann Cruyff, Maradonna, Zine-dine Zidane, Wayne Rooney, Ronaldo and Lionel Messi at their peaks and all rolled into one. I'd also wished I could run at twice my normal speed. This meant I could run the 100 metres in a fraction over 6 seconds, so I didn't reckon anyone was going to do me for pace.

I spotted Mum and Dad and Emily up in the Executive Box. I waved. They waved back. Claire and Natalie were in the crowd somewhere, too. So were Dirk and Shushmita with the rest of Kiss My Chuddies. So were Steve Renwick and his followers. I'd wished for them to come along just to rub their noses in it. I'd even wished for Mr Tubby to be here. He was sitting in the Coronation Gardens end, looking slightly out of place in his suit and tie. Everyone I wanted to impress was here.

And man, was I going to impress them.

The opposition today was Torquay United. Just before kick-off, the Torquay centre back, who'd be marking me (yeah, right), came up and eyeballed me. He was a big ugly guy with a broken nose and sort of splintery teeth.

'Debut today, is it, sonny?'

'That's right.'

'Break a leg!' He laughed in a sort of menacing manner.

Stupid twat.

I decided he'd pay for trying to intimidate me.

The whistle blew. Torquay kicked off – but with the speed of a cheetah in full flight I raced in and whisked the ball off the forward's toes. And I was off, heading down the centre of the pitch towards the Torquay goal.

The ugly centre back with the broken nose and the splintery teeth loomed up and aimed a savage hack at my knees. With contemptuous ease I stepped over the challenge, and carried along by his own impetus he fell flat on his face.

I stopped and put my foot on the ball, waiting for him to get up.

He scrambled to his feet and rushed at me, this time aiming a kick at my ankle.

I dodged nimbly to the side, flipping the ball along with me.

Again, I stood and waited for him to have another go. I felt like a matador playing with a bull. He gave this kind of bellow of rage and just ran straight at me, trying to barge me over. I stepped gracefully aside and, unable to stop himself, he went charging off the pitch and crashed into the hoardings at the side. The crowd went wild.

Other Torquay players were homing in on me now. I just dribbled through them as if they were traffic cones.

Now I was on the edge of the box. The goalie was coming out with this kind of desperate look on his face. In full flight, without checking my stride, I rifled a long, low shot past him, straight into the bottom right corner of the net. It went so fast he didn't even see it. He looked round and the net was bulging.

The crowd are going absolutely wild. I race back to my half, my hand up, my finger pointing to the heavens to salute my brilliant goal. My team-mates are all running to congratulate me, but of course they can't get anywhere near me. After a bit I slow down and let them catch me, so they can hug me and ruffle my hair and all that stuff. Torquay just stand around looking stunned.

That set the pattern for the game, really. Every few minutes I'd get the ball and bang in another spectacular goal. My favourite was a diving header from my own cross.

The Torquay manager pulled his centre back off at half-time. (All right, stop laughing, you know what I mean.) But the replacement, obviously, didn't have any more success. Long before the end, the Torquay team looked like men living through a nightmare. The final score was 7–0.

I could have scored a lot more, of course, but I decided to exercise a bit of what you might call artistic restraint.

'Wow! Adam, you were amazing!'

'Yes, I know.'

Claire had come round to see me after the match. She'd brought a big bunch of flowers and a bottle of champagne. I was getting a bit sick of that stuff to be honest. She hadn't brought Natalie, though.

'What about Natalie? What did she think of it?'

Claire's face sort of crumpled. 'Why are you asking that? Why are you always asking about Natalie?'

She looked like she was going to cry and I couldn't stand that. I put my arms around her but she was as stiff as a goalpost. I was like, 'I wish you'd forget what I just said,' and she sighed and softened herself against me.

'What did you say just now?'

'I said thanks for the flowers, they're really nice.'

There was a knock at the front door. My heart jumped like a frog – no, scrub that, it doesn't sound very romantic, let's say it leaped like a salmon. I ran downstairs. I thought maybe it was Natalie, you see. But it wasn't. When I opened the door there were these two guys standing there. One of them had a camera.

'We're from the Waltham Forest Guardian,' said the one without the camera. He had this kind of nasal voice. 'Could we talk to you for a few minutes? Get a few pictures?'

'Yeah, why not? Come in.'

'That was an amazing performance today, Mr Gowers.'

'Call me Adam.'

'That was an amazing performance today, Adam.'

'Thanks.'

Then Claire appeared at the top of the stairs.

'It's the local paper – they've come to interview me.'

'Who's this?' goes the guy without the camera.

'It's my, er, you know, it's my, it's Claire, she's my, well, my, er, girlfriend, really.'

'Oh, lovely, let's get a few shots of you and the girlfriend. Come along, Claire, stand there, that's right, put your arm round her, Adam… Lovely, that's right… And again… And another…'

Claire was loving this, I could tell. Her face was all lit up like a Christmas tree.

'Now for a few questions. Adam, you scored seven goals today – did you know that was a record for a debut?'

'Well, I kind of thought it might be.'

'Where did you learn to play like that?'

'It's just a knack.'

The guy laughed nasally. 'Some knack! Tell me, what do you plan to do with this knack? What are your ambitions?'

'First, I wanna get Orient promoted. After that, we'll see.'

'Are you hoping to move to a bigger club?'

'No, I'll stay with the O's. They're the team I've always supported and it's a, like, honour to play for them.'

'Lovely, lovely. OK, we've got what we need. It'll be in on Thursday, OK?'

The door closed behind them.

Claire was like, 'You don't think I'll look fat in that photo, do you?'

'No, cause you're not fat. You'll look beautiful. Cause you are beautiful.'

'No I'm not!' But she was smiling. Her face was all aglow. In fact she looked really pretty. It made me wonder why I was so horrible to her.

I was like, 'Shall we go and have a, like, lie-down?'

'Sure!' Claire giggled. 'You've scored seven times today. Why not make it eight?' And she gave a wicked little smile.

I have to say, as wicked little smiles go, it was right up there with Natalie's.

That Waltham Forest Guardian piece was the first of many. After the next match at Boreham Wood, where I banged in another seven goals, the nationals got interested. I had journalists from *The Sun*, *The Mirror*, *The Daily Express*, *The Daily Mail*, *The Times*, *The Telegraph* and *The Guardian* all coming round and asking the same questions. The one in the *Mail* had a cute picture of me playing football in the garden with Emily. But my favourite one of all was in *The Mercury*. She was called Samuella Johnson, the journalist who interviewed me – which made a change because it was mostly men who came to interview me – and I enjoyed the interview because she acted like she really fancied me. Kind of flirtatious. I had a sort of idea, even at the time, that she was putting on an act just to get a good interview, but I still enjoyed it. This is what she wrote:

BOY WONDER

If I had a daughter, I'd want her to marry Adam Gowers. No, I wouldn't, I'd be green with jealousy. I want him for myself. Adam Gowers is totally, completely, utterly, drop-dead gorgeous. Six foot two with eyes of green. A god-like physique and cheekbones to die for. It was all I could do to prevent my tongue hanging out.

Adam Gowers, in case you've been on the moon these last couple of weeks, is the latest football superstar to emerge from East London. Once we had David Beckham from Leytonstone, now we have Adam Gowers from Walthamstow. I asked Adam what he thought of Becks.

'He was a good player, in his day.'

'Better than you?'

'It's kind of early to say. But I reckon I can achieve what he's achieved and more.'

These are brave words from a 17-year-old who's played only two games for the unfashionable League Two side Leyton Orient. To be honest, when I first heard the name Leyton Orient, I assumed it must be an Asian supermarket. But Adam's first two games were no ordinary games, by all accounts. He scored fourteen goals, seven in each. Even I know that's pretty amazing.

I once heard a footballer say that scoring goals was better than sex. If that's true, Adam must be drunk with ecstasy the whole time. Also pretty tired. Well?

At this point, Adam does something rather charming. He blushes. A warm red glow steals across his handsome features. He has a man's body, but he's a boy at heart. 'Er – I wouldn't say that scoring goals is better than sex. The two activities are totally different.'

Well, I wouldn't disagree there. So, can he keep it up? Sorry, sorry, I didn't mean that double entendre. Not consciously, anyway. I can't answer for my unconscious mind. It can be naughty at times.

At my question he blushes again. I seem to be rather good at making Adam blush. I wonder if I can do it fourteen times.

'If you mean can I keep on scoring goals, yeah, I reckon I can. That's what I plan to do, anyway.'

At the same prodigious rate?

For a moment I think 'prodigious' might be too much for a 17-year-old boy from Walthamstow. But this is the boy who got four A-star grades in his AS levels. Brains as well as beauty. It's just not fair.

'Yeah, I reckon I'll carry on scoring at the same rate. Maybe it'll get even more prodigious.'

If it does, the big clubs will be after him. Will he follow Becks to Manchester United or Real Madrid?

'No. I'm going stay where I am. Orient are my local club. I've always supported them. My plan is to get us promoted till we're in the Premiership. Then we're going to win the European Championship.'

He has it all mapped out, I see. Beauty, brains, talent and a career plan. He's too good for my daughter. Not that I've got a daughter. But perhaps I could have one? With Adam? No, no, I must stop being so naughty. I bet Adam has a girlfriend, doesn't he?

'Yeah,' he says, lapsing into teenage monosyllabic mode.

Does he have a picture?

He shows me a picture on his phone of a rather pretty, healthy-looking teenager with blonde hair. And what's her name, Adam?

'Claire.'

Lucky Claire. I feel a disturbing pang of jealousy as I look at her smiling features. I hand the photo back before my emotions get the better of me and make me tear it to shreds.

This boy's got the lot. Beauty, brains, talent, a career plan, a pretty teenage girlfriend – and soon he's going to be very, very rich. What's he going to do with all the money? Is he going to buy his parents a mansion in Essex?

'I might. Doesn't have to be Essex.'

No, indeed. So what else will he buy? A flash car to drive Claire around in?

'Got one already. A Porsche. It's outside.'

I run to the window and there, parked outside Adam's

ordinary, not particularly posh terraced house, is a gleaming silver Porsche. I can't believe I didn't notice it before. It stands out like a yacht on a duck pond.

I'd better be going, before I lose my heart entirely.

Well, goodbye, Adam. We shake hands. He has a strong, firm, masculine grip. Thanks for the interview.

'Thank you. I enjoyed it.'

He gives me a shatteringly beautiful, warm, boyish open smile. Quick, I must leave or I'll never get out of here!

As I pass the silver Porsche outside, I think, there is a boy on whom the gods have smiled. I hope they keep smiling. That way, I may be back to interview him again.

Samuella Johnson

Claire liked this piece, too. Well, she liked it up to a point. She liked being mentioned, because in some of them she wasn't. And I thought she'd like being called pretty, but she didn't.

'It says *rather* pretty. That means not pretty at all!'

'No it doesn't, it just means pretty.'

'If she'd meant pretty she'd have just said pretty, not put in *rather*. And what's this about "healthy-looking"? That means fat!'

'If she'd meant fat she'd have just said fat.'

'No she wouldn't. "Healthy-looking" is a code for fat, everyone knows that!'

'Well, I didn't.'

Claire snorted. 'Every girl knows what it means. She's a cow. It sounds like she was coming on to you like mad!'

'Nah, it was all part of the act, it didn't mean anything.'

Claire looked at Samuella's picture at the top of the article. She had her head on one side and this sort of cute smile. Samuella did, I mean, not Claire. Claire was like, 'Look at that! What a tart!'

'Oh, she was all right.'

'How can you say that? She was horrible!'

'You never met her.'

'No, thank God!'

I could see, in a way, why Claire was worried. It must have been hard, the way her boyfriend was suddenly an overnight superstar, in all the papers and stuff. She was worried she was going to lose me.

I put my arms round her. 'Don't worry,' I said. 'I won't leave you.'

'What?' Again she imitated a goalpost. 'Who said anything about leaving me?'

'I said I won't.'

'But why did you say even say that? You must be thinking of it!'

This was getting out of control. There was only one thing to do.

'I wish you'd be happy again. And I wish you'd forget this conversation.'

'What conversation?'

'I dunno! Let's go out for a pizza.'

We went out for a pizza.

CHAPTER 9

Scoring goals for the O's was brilliant, but as time went by it gradually got less and less brilliant, until one day it wasn't brilliant at all.

It wasn't even fairly good.

In fact it was crap.

It was in a game at Aldershot, on a damp and chilly October day, that I realised I was totally fed up with the whole pathetic charade. Orient were top of the division by miles and Aldershot were somewhere between the middle and the bottom. At this point, I had an average of 8.8 goals per game. Even before the whistle blew, I could see the Aldershot players eyeing me fearfully. As soon as the game started, I got the ball and sprinted towards the Aldershot goal. The Aldershot players tried their best to tackle me, but their best was like the best of a three-year-old kid in the park trying to tackle his dad. I blasted the ball into the net. The ref blew the whistle. The small contingent of O's fans in the crowd cheered. The Aldershot supporters were silent and looked totally gutted. So did the Aldershot players. It was only half a minute into the game and they were already a goal down. They knew, every one of them, that they were in for a record hammering in front of their home crowd.

The O's players mumbled congratulations. I could tell that even they weren't overwhelmed about it. It was all getting too predictable. The team was like a one-man band. They had to congratulate me about nine times a game and they were getting bored with it. And so was I. It was boring the arse off me, if you'll pardon my French.

Well, I knocked in another five goals before half time. I wasn't enjoying it any more and I felt pretty sorry for Aldershot. I mean, what had they ever done to me? But... it was my job to score goals. If I didn't score them it was a waste of time being here. I did try and set Sammy Pollock up for a goal, to introduce a bit of variety. But the talentless clot kept blasting the ball wide or over the bar.

We trooped into the dressing room at half-time and Barry

Blodger gave us the usual pep talk. 'Great work, lads, keep it up. I reckon this one's in the bag.' What else could he say? We sat in silence for most of the break and ate our oranges.

And this was it, this was my life now, banging in goals against crap National League teams every Saturday. And next season, I'd be doing the same against slightly less crap League Two teams in the English Football League. Then a season banging them in against League One teams. Then another season serving time in the Championship. And then there'd be the Premiership, and I'd have to spend a whole season winning that. And then another season playing against the top European teams. It was a long time to wait to lift the European Cup. Christ, it was going to take six years!

Of course, I could have speeded up the process by getting a transfer to a Premiership club. There'd been no shortage of offers. The phone didn't stop ringing at home. I'd had offers from Man United, Man City, Arsenal, Chelsea, Liverpool and Tottenham Hotspur. Martin had been in touch and said I should join him at Arsenal but I didn't want to do that – I was so much better than him that it would have taken the shine off his achievement in making the first team. I'd end up turning him and the rest of the team into cheerleaders for my one-man band. That may be what Miss Rogers would call a mixed metaphor but you know what I mean. So I'd said thanks but no thanks to all the big clubs who were chasing me.

It was kind of funny, the way they just couldn't believe I'd rather play for Orient. They offered me ridiculous amounts of money. Like they'd go, 'A hundred million, and that really is our last word, take it or leave it,' and I'd be like, 'OK, I'll leave it then,' and they'd be like 'OK, then, a hundred and ten million!'

The money meant nothing to me – I could just wish for it, after all, if that was what I wanted. It's true it might have been a little bit more fun to play for a top club. You get a better class of opposition. But my plan, the whole point of it, was for Orient to lift the European Cup, not Man City or Chelsea. It was just a pity it was going to take six years.

And then I had an idea. A brainwave. Or that's what I thought.

Why *should* I have to wait six years? I could have whatever I wanted, whenever I wanted.

'Right, lads,' goes Barry Blodger, as the half-time break came to an end. 'Second half – get out there and do it to them again! You know the drill – get the ball to Adam whenever you can.'

As we're going down the tunnel, I'm like, 'I wish we were just about to start the European Cup Final.'

And everything changed.

The first thing I noticed was the weather. The grey October clamminess lifted. Suddenly it was a glorious, golden sunny day. And the noise. Instead of the muttering Aldershot crowd there was a huge wall of sound as we ran out onto the pitch; not Aldershot's pitch, but the giant bowl of the San Siro stadium, packed to the top with cheering, roaring fans. Blimey. I turned round to say 'Blimey' to Sammy Pollock but he'd gone. I didn't recognise any of my teammates now. They'd been replaced by a bunch of lean and powerful athletes. I was different, too. I felt bigger, stronger, fitter. I was wearing a different strip as well. It was still an O's kit, but it had been redesigned with little stripes and splotches on it and it was made of some kind of shiny material. Sponsored by Microsoft.

It was weird. Here I was in the European Cup Final against Juventus. I only knew that cause it said so on the giant electronic scoreboard. I didn't have a clue who we'd beaten to get here.

Anyhow. Juventus kicked off and passed the ball about for a bit. After a while I got fed up waiting for the ball so I nipped in and tackled a Juve player and headed off for goal. Immediately I had, like, four Juve players on me. They obviously had me marked down as the danger man. And they were right.

But there was nothing they could do – I skipped over their tackles and once I was away, well, they might as well have tried to catch a greyhound. The keeper came rushing out. I could see the despair on his face. He must have watched videos of me in team training, slotting in goals at will against the finest keepers in Europe, and now it was his turn. I chipped the ball over his head. A beautiful, precision chip, hit with just enough weight to take it clear of his clawing hands, but let it come down in time to dip under the bar and roll gently down the back of the net.

The Orient fans cheered. The Juve fans booed. The Juve players looked pissed off and resigned. Just like the Aldershot players had, really. And my team-mates acted just like the old Orient players, that is, they congratulated me but with zero enthusiasm. They must have been getting fed up with it, too.

As for me... well, I felt nothing at all. I didn't get any sense of triumph from the goal. It was just too easy. I was *too* good – Juve or Aldershot, it made no difference, I could score whenever I felt like it. There's no point in football when it's like that. It's completely no fun.

Suddenly, I felt sick of the whole thing. I just couldn't be bothered to play out the remaining eighty-six minutes. What was the point? I'd score another seven goals, or eight, or twenty if I felt like it, and by the final whistle all the Juve fans would have gone home and the Juve players would be wishing they could do the same, and everyone in the world who'd been watching would have switched off their telly long ago, except for O's fans, and maybe even they'd have got bored with it – and my team-mates would be thinking, what's the point of this, we needn't even have bothered to turn up when Adam can win the game on his own.

I was like, 'I wish the game was over and we'd won 1–0.'

And the next second I found myself facing the other goal and the ref was blowing his whistle. The giant electronic scoreboard said Orient 1, Juventus 0.

Then I'm going up the steps to collect the trophy, and I hold it above my head, and there's cameras flashing and cheering from the O's fans. This is the moment I've been waiting for. The O's have won the European Cup.

But...

So what?

The way I feel, I might as well be holding up a tea-cup or an egg-cup. It's cost me no effort at all to get to this moment. I'm not even sweating. And take it from me, there's no fun whatsoever in winning a trophy under those conditions.

And now, I suppose, I've got to go back to some hotel and tomorrow get on a plane and fly back to London and a shedload of reporters will greet me at the airport. They won't greet the other O's players, though. They won't even notice them. I wonder what the O's players think of me? I bet they hate my guts. I mean, I would.

I feel like I just want to get out of there. I'm not going do the hotel/plane/reporters bit. Just not gonna do it, man. I'm like, 'I wish I was home.'

The scene changes like a cut in a film. The stadium and the cheering crowd are gone. It's a quiet, summer evening, all I can hear is a few birds singing.

And I'm in front of a house I've never seen before in my life.

CHAPTER 10

I'm standing on the drive of a big mansion in the countryside. Well, it's sort of like the country, there's green spaces and trees all round, but there's other mansions, too. In the distance. Like pieces on a giant green chessboard.

What the hell's going on? This isn't my house. It's got steps going up to this great big porch with columns, like some sort of Greek temple or something. There's a massive drive with four cars parked in it: a white Jag and a red Lamborghini, plus my silver Porsche and my funky little jeep. So maybe it is my house after all.

I go up to the front door, but I don't have any keys to get in. I'm still wearing my Orient strip, of course. So I knock on the door.

I'm expecting to see Mum or Dad, but when the door swings open who should I see but Claire.

In fact, I'm not sure at first if it is Claire or just someone who looks like her. She's changed a lot. She looks older. She's slimmer. Tanned. She's had her hair done in this kind of feathery style and it's dyed or bleached so it's paler than before. She's wearing black trousers and a black silk shirt and a gold necklace. She looks dead rich. And she's carrying a small suitcase.

'Er – Claire?'

I've read in books about people whose eyes blaze. I never really knew what it meant before. I mean, how can eyes blaze? They don't catch fire, do they? But now, for the first time, I understand the expression. That's what Claire's eyes do when they look at me. They blaze.

'What are you doing in your football kit?'

'I've just been playing in a match. It was the European Cup Final.'

'You – you're just a rat, aren't you? The papers were right. You're a rat!'

'Wodjer mean?' I was stunned. 'What are you talking about? Course I'm not a rat.'

'I just can't believe it. I can't believe your total insensitivity!'

'What? What have I done?'

'This is just – it's clutching at the last straw!'

'You don't need to say clutching. That's a different expression, clutching at straws. What you mean is, it's the last straw.'

'All I know is, it's the tin lid!'

'But what is? I don't even know what's going on!'

'I'll tell you what's going on. It's over. Finished. Dead as a duck!'

'What? What's finished?'

Claire skewers me with a grey-eyed glare. 'Why don't you take a good, long hard look at yourself, Adam? Just look at your life. When did you last do anything for anyone except yourself? You're a selfish egotistical narcissist, living in a little bubble where all that matters is getting what you want – satisfying your appetites! You're not a man, just a willy and a stomach on legs!'

'Look, can you just explain? Do we live here?'

'Not any more!'

She flounces past me and gets into the Jag.

'Where are you going?'

She's like, 'Away from you!' Then she bursts into tears.

She drives away with tears streaming down her cheeks and the windscreen wipers going, for some reason.

Well, go figure. She must have gone crazy, that was the only explanation. Flipped her lid. Lost her marbles. Destination funny farm. Unless… it was *me*? Maybe *I'd* gone crazy. I didn't have a clue what was going on.

I went into the house. It was a pretty cool place. Wooden floors and velvet sofas, a staircase wide enough to lie down on. There was a great big garden with a swimming pool glinting bluely in it. I felt like that guy on 'Through the Keyhole'. 'Whoever lives here has plenty of money,' you know the sort of thing. I went into this room with a great big shiny polished wooden dining table. On the table was a newspaper. It caught my eye because there was a photo of me on the front page.

I picked it up. There I was, leaving some sort of nightclub with a fruity beauty on my arm. The headline said: 'ADAM'S MADAM'. Underneath it said: 'I shagged top model in my Orient kit!'

Oh.

Right.

I started to get a glimmering of why the sight of me in my O's strip had annoyed Claire so much.

But I still didn't really get it. I looked for my phone, couldn't find it, wished for it and phoned Dirk.

'The number you have dialled has not been recognised...'

He must have changed his phone. Well, I knew his old landline number so I tried that.

'Hello?' That was Dirk's mum.

'Hi – is Dirk there?'

'Who is this?'

'It's Adam.'

'Oh, Adam.' Her voice was surprised, but it was a cold, displeased surprise. She couldn't have sounded more unwelcoming if I'd been a double-glazing salesman. 'Well, Dirk's not here, of course.'

'Oh, right. Do you know when he'll be back?'

'No. Not till Christmas, I expect.'

'What?'

'Goodbye, Adam.'

'Wait – where is he?'

'He's in the States. As well you know.'

'What's he doing there?'

'Goodbye.'

'No, wait – have you got his number there?'

'If you want his number, you'd better ask him yourself.'

'But how *can* I –?'

Too late. She'd put the phone down. Stupid old trout. I just couldn't work out what was going on. It seemed like suddenly everyone really disliked me. And I always used to get on really well with Dirk's mum. I used to make her laugh. Now it seemed more like I made her sick.

Anyway, it didn't matter that she wouldn't give me Dirk's number. I only had to wish for it. So I did, and then I dialled it.

'Hi, Dirk!'

There was a pause. Then Dirk was like, 'Hey, is that Adam?' He sounded surprised, too, but a bit friendlier than his mum.

'Yeah, it's me.'

'Long time since I heard from you.'

'Is it?'

'You know it is.'

'I don't, honest. I seem to have sort of lost my memory or something. Like, what are you doing in the States?'

'I'm at Cornell University. Studying philosophy. And teaching it, too.'

'What? But how did that happen?'

'Well, after my degree I did an MA and then I applied to do a PhD here and they've given me some lecturing work, too.'

'But how can you be lecturing at your age?'

'What do you mean? I'm 23. OK, that's a little bit young to be lecturing, but it's not –'

'You're 23?'

'Of course I am, same as you!'

'Blimey. What about Shushmita, what's she been doing?'

'She's here too. In fact I applied to Cornell partly because of her. Her band got a recording contract in the States. They're doing really well over here. But you must know all this. What's the matter, man? Are you on something?'

'No, no, nothing like that. Look, I made this wish that I was in the European Cup Final, right, and the next minute, six years has just, like, disappeared.'

'You can't remember anything of the last six years?'

'As far as I'm concerned there hasn't *been* a last six years.'

'Hmmm...' goes Dirk. I can just imagine him raising his eyebrows quizzically. I bet he still does that.

'Look,' I go. 'What's going on?'

'This really is extraordinarily interesting,' goes Dirk, slowly and thoughtfully. 'I tell you what's happened. I think. You wished to be in the final, right, so your wish just threw you forward six years in time – that's how long it would take before Orient could be in the final, right? But everyone else lived through those six years in the normal way.'

'But what about me? Where was I?'

'Well, you were certainly around,' goes Dirk. He sounds intensely pensive. I bet he talks like that in his philosophy classes and all the girls fancy him for being such an intellectual. 'This is the interesting bit. Because you didn't just disappear off the face of the earth for six years. There *was* a you, doing all the stuff you were doing – but you can't remember it, because from your point of view you didn't actually live through it. Your subjective experience doesn't match up with what objectively happened.'

'Well, what have I been doing for six years, then? Apart from playing football.'

Dirk laughed. 'You don't wanna know, man.'

'No, I *do* wanna know!'

'Well… there's quite a lot to tell. Why don't you just wish you knew?'

'Oh yeah, right.'

I wished. And a flood of memories came pouring into my brain.

It was weird, like my brain was a bathtub with this stream of multi-coloured pictures swirling into it from a tap. Me getting thrown out of nightclubs. Trashing hotel bedrooms. Trashing nightclubs. Getting thrown out of hotels. Spending whole days in restaurants eating my way through the menu. Drinking whole crates of champagne. Snorting blizzards of coke. Having parties that lasted weeks. Parties on yachts, parties on private jets. And always a different woman hanging onto my arm – and always a beautiful one. Models, film stars, pop stars. I'd had a bit of a fling with that Samuella Johnson, too, when she came back to interview me again after Orient got in the Premiership. That was the one that pissed Claire off most of all. Tabloid headlines all about me – ADAM SCORES AGAIN, ANOTHER EVE FOR ADAM, WOULD YOU ADAM AND EVE IT? – crap jokes like that. And Claire hanging round in the background, looking kind of sick. It was a wonder she'd put up with me for so long.

It seemed like I'd been what they call a bit of a hell-raiser and a love rat. The funny thing was, running through all these memories, I didn't get any impression that I'd been happy raising hell and being a love rat. The impression I got was of a constant battle against being bored. And a losing battle, what's more. And what's even more, I knew why.

It was Natalie, of course. All those girls meant nothing. Zero. They were pathetic, desperate attempts to make up for the one thing I couldn't have. Natalie being in love with me. If you'd offered me that – Natalie really loving me, of her own free will – I'd have swapped all my wishes for it, no question. But that wasn't going to happen, was it? I got that terrible pain again just thinking about it, a big sharp pin stuck in my big swollen red heart.

And I didn't even have Claire as a consolation any more.

I thought of Dirk. He had a beautiful girlfriend he was mad about. She hadn't walked out on him, like Claire had just walked out on me. And she was a pop star, for Christ's sake. That was pretty annoying. In a way it was all my fault – I'd pushed him towards Shushmita cause of wishing Natalie would never go out with him – but that didn't stop it being annoying. In fact it made it more annoying. And then, Dirk was doing obviously pretty well for himself in his career. To be lecturing at Cornell University at 23 he must be quite a hot-shot. And he loved his job, while I was sick of mine. He got paid good money for spouting off about the meaning of life, which he'd have been perfectly happy to do for nothing. Do it for nothing? He'd have *paid* to do it. He'd had a much better six years than me. And *I* was the one with the wishes.

It was pretty sickening.

'Well?' goes Dirk. 'Has it all come back to you?'

I'm like, 'Blimey.'

'Yeah, blimey,' agreed Dirk. 'You have been busy.'

'Yeah, busy having a crap time. What's gone wrong? Why aren't I enjoying my wishes like I should?'

'You know what Aristotle said?'

'Yeah, he said "Lend us a tenner till Thursday, mate".'

'He said –'

'I don't wanna know what some stupid old dead Greek said. I just wanna know how to be happy.'

'I reckon you need to stop trying so hard to be happy. Why don't you try being altruistic?'

'Altruistic, huh?'

'It means doing stuff for other people. Not for yourself.'

'Yeah, I do know what it means, actually. Just cause I'm a foot-baller doesn't mean I'm thick.'

'OK. OK. Anyway, why don't you give it a go? Help the world. Think of all you could do! Like, stop famines and wars and so forth, instead of getting chucked out of nightclubs.'

I didn't say anything for a bit. Then I was like, 'Yeah, maybe. I'll think about it.'

'Good. Hey, look, why don't you come over to the States? It'd be good to see you again.'

'I'll think about it. Yeah, maybe.'

I didn't go to the States, though. There wouldn't have been any point cause Dirk wasn't there any more. Not after I'd made my next wish. I made it as soon as I put the phone down. I wished the last six years hadn't happened. Just wished them away, into oblivion. I wished I was still 17. I didn't want to be 23. I wasn't up for it. I wasn't ready.

So everything was back like it had been after the Aldershot game. Dirk was a schoolboy again and Shushmita hadn't yet got her recording contract in the States. I didn't have a mansion in the coun-try and Claire hadn't just walked out of it. And Emily was three years old again, not nine. And none of them would ever know they'd lived through six years and then had them wiped clean away.

It was kind of a weird thought.

So there I was, 17 years old again. I lay on my bed and tried to work out what to do. It got dark but I didn't put the light on. The moon shone in through a chink in the curtains.

I thought hard. I wanted to get the next six years right this time.

Maybe I'd give up being a footballer. Been there, done that, got the medal. But what would I do instead?

Be altruistic, Dirk had said. Well... maybe there was something in that.

The only thing was, where should I start? There was so much crap going on in the world. It was too much. To get a handle on it, I wished for a newspaper – *The Mercury*, I kind of liked that since Samuella Johnson's piece – and flicked through it.

Guy on holiday in Majorca falls off balcony on his bonce. Journalist kidnapped in Philippines. Ferry sinks off Indonesia. Executions in Katmandu. Shooting in Northern Ireland. Floods in Bangladesh. AIDS on the increase throughout Africa. Drought in the Sudan. High School massacre in USA. Suicide bombers blow up pizza restaurant in Tel Aviv. Israeli tanks roll into Palestinian town. Honour killing in Bradford. Acid attacks in Pakistan. Neo-Nazis on the rampage in Rome. Crazy cult members top themselves in Peru. Some guy gets his nose cut off in Ecuador. Bloke gets eye gouged out on London bus.

All over the world, wherever you looked, some sort of shit was going down. How was I going to sort all this out? Should I wish everyone who'd just got killed was alive again? But I couldn't keep doing that. Every day more people were going get wasted, I'd never keep up with it.

Suppose I wished no one would ever die again? No, that would be rubbish, the world would get seriously overpopulated in no time. We'd be bursting at the seams. Unless I wished people would stop having babies? No, that wouldn't be good, people like babies. Everyone likes babies. Babies are nice.

What about the floods in Bangladesh? Maybe I should wish it would stop raining. But then they might get a drought. What about the drought in the Sudan? Maybe I should wish for it to start raining. But then they might get a flood...

Whatever I wished for, it was going to have *consequences*. And then I'd have to wish again to sort out the consequences, and wish again to sort out the consequences of sorting out the consequences. And all the time new crap would be happening all over the world. It was going to be a lifetime's work to sort it all out. I'd have to give up eating and sleeping and going to the toilet to keep track of it.

What I needed was one simple wish, one wish that would wrap everything up and then it would be sorted once and for all. What was everyone's problem, when you got right down to it? Everyone's problem was that they were unhappy, right?

So...

A giant light-bulb lit up over my head.

Not literally, I mean, it's a metaphor, like Miss Rogers is always going on about in English. What if I wished everyone was permanently happy?

It had to be for always, because I knew from experience that when I wished about people's moods, the wish came true but it tended to wear off after a bit, if there were underlying factors to return it to default. Like when I wished my mum and dad would kiss and make up – well, they did, but it didn't last because deep down they had too many grudges against each other. But if I keyed it into the wish that it would last for the rest of everyone's lives – that guaranteed everyone would be happy and stay happy.

Except for me. I'd better leave myself out of the wish, otherwise it wouldn't really be altruistic.

It's true that I'd made a resolve not to interfere with other people's emotions. But, you know, resolutions are made to be broken. This seemed like a cool idea to me.

And if it went tits-up? Suppose people didn't *like* being happy all the time? But of course they'd like being happy all the time, who wouldn't? How could you *not* be happy about being happy? No, I couldn't see anything wrong with the wish.

And anyway – this was the really cool bit – if there *was* something wrong with it, something I hadn't thought of, all I had to do was unwish it again, like I did with Bobbligrubs talking.

OK, then. No problem.

'I wish everyone in the world was happy for the rest of their lives, except me.'

That was it, then. I'd done it. I'd put an end to human misery.

Once and for all. Kind of a historic day, really. It was like a fairy story. 'And they all lived happily ever after.'

After that, I came over all tired. I'd had a pretty busy day. If I'd kept a diary, I'd have been able to make quite a spectacular diary entry.

'18 October. Travelled forward six years in time and won European Cup. Came back again and ended human misery forever.'

I got into bed and pulled the covers over my head.

In a few seconds, I was fast asleep.

CHAPTER 11

I was woken up the next day by the sound of my dad singing, 'Oh, What a Beautiful Mornin'.'

He thinks he's a brilliant singer, my dad. You can tell he's really proud of his voice, the way he wobbles on the high notes, and goes to a sort of deep growl for the low ones. And he puts on an embarrassing phony American accent for singing pop songs. Normally it annoys the hell out of me. But today I didn't mind. The guy was happy, why shouldn't he sing? It showed my wish was kicking in.

Then I heard my mum joining in. Or not joining in, exactly, cause she was singing, 'If You're Happy and You Know It.'

And then Emily piped up with, 'Old MacDonald Had a Farm.'

I wished I was washed and dressed in the twinkling of an eye, as usual, and went downstairs. They were all in the kitchen, singing away like they were auditioning for *The X Factor*. But they stopped when they saw me. Their faces lit up with pleasure. Emily clapped her hands. It was kind of nice to see.

'Morning, Adam!'

'Hi.'

'Isn't it a lovely day?'

I looked out of the window. Rain was drizzling down from a yellowish-grey sky.

'Wodjer mean, lovely day? It's raining.'

'Ah, yes, but it's good for the farmers!' goes my dad.

'And think how grateful all the little ponds and streams and rivers will be, to be topped up by the rain!' goes my mum.

'Yeah, right.'

Inspired by this, Emily started singing a nonsense song about rain at the top of her voice. 'Wain, wain, wain, wain in the sky, wain in your eye, wain in your pie...'

Inspired in his turn, my dad started on 'American Pie' in his best 'aren't-I-a-great-singer' voice. He stopped at the chorus to say, 'I used to sing for the county, you know!' Then he carried on.

Then my mum started singing to me, like a character in a musical. 'Would you like some toast, Adam, would you like some tea? Would you like an egg, Adam, would that be lovelee?'

'Tea and toast'd be fine, Mum.'

'Fine, fine, fine! A piece of toast for the one I love most!'

'Give the lad some Marmite on it!'

'I don't want Marmite, thanks.' (I don't hate Marmite, by the way. Or love it. I just think it's fairly nice every now and again, but I didn't fancy any today.)

'In that case, hold the Marmite!' goes my dad, and they all laughed as if he'd said something hilarious.

'Give him JAM!' goes Emily at the top of her voice. They all laughed again.

I drank my tea and scoffed my toast pretty quick. It was good to see them all so happy, but I could imagine how in the long run it could get kind of wearing. They had these fixed, bright smiles on and everything they said sounded like it had an exclamation mark after it. I might have to wish to tone them down a bit, if this carried on. They reminded me of some Evangelical Christians who came and stood outside our school with leaflets one time and asked everyone if they wanted to be born again. No thanks, mate. Once is enough, I reckon.

'I don't know what's got into me today!' goes my dad. 'I just feel so wonderfully happy! I've got Mrs Sprocket this morning – and I don't mind a bit! In fact I'm looking forward to it!'

'Oh, but wait a minute!' goes my mum. 'You don't normally have Mrs Sprocket today!'

'She booked an extra session!'

'But you know I'm working at the library today! Who's going to look after Emily?'

Emily looked from one to the other, smiling. 'Yes, who's going to look after me?'

This was just the kind of thing that in the old days would have caused World War 3 to break out. But today, the smiles never left their faces.

'We'll sort it out somehow!'

'I could cancel my session at the library!'

'Or I could put Mrs Sprocket off!'

I was like, 'It's OK. I'll take Emily out with me.'

'Would you really?' goes my mum. 'That would be wonderful!'

'He's a wonderful son!'

'And a wonderful brother!'

'He's just all-round wonderful!'

'He's a wonderful watering-can!' goes Emily. She's at this stage where she thinks it's really funny to use the wrong words on purpose.

'Morning Adam!'

That was George Morrance, our next-door-neighbour, giving me a cheery wave. Pretty amazing, really, because normally he's the most bad-tempered git who ever stomped over the surface the earth.

Not any more, though. There aren't any bad-tempered people left, now. I've abolished them. The whole category of Bad-Tempered-Git is no more.

Emily toddled along beside me down the street.

'Come on, Em – let's go for a ride.'

'Are we going for a ride in a plane?'

'No, in my car.'

'In a ship?'

'No, in my car.'

'On a woller-skate?'

'No, in my car.'

'In a space ship?'

'Yeah, OK, in a space ship – let's go to Mars, eh?'

We'd reached my funky little orange and green jeep. Emily laughed and kicked her legs as I strapped her into the car seat.

I thought it would be good to drive into the centre of London and see what it looked like when it was full of happy people. It had stopped raining now and the sun was coming out. The wet pavements glistened. But not as brightly as the smiles of the people. Everywhere you looked – in shops, at bus stops, crossing zebra crossings – people had these great big cheesy grins on. They looked like they all had a slice of melon wedged sideways across their mouths.

And do you know what, I'm starting to get a bit fed up with it already. It's like the city's been taken over by androids.

I might have to have a radical rethink on this one.

Then I suddenly spot Natalie, Claire and Shushmita walking along Hoe Street. I get this sort of sweet juicy pain in my heart – that's cause of seeing Natalie – and almost at the same time my guts give this sort of twist – that's cause of seeing Claire, cause I do really like her and I feel guilty about all that love-rat stuff I did when I was a famous footballer, even though she doesn't know anything about it, cause as far as she's concerned it hasn't happened – and then I get this slight kind of lurching feeling inside – that's cause of seeing Shushmita, cause I feel a bit jealous of her for going to be a pop star and a bit jealous of Dirk for going out with her.

So, all in all, quite a reaction to just seeing three girls walking down the street.

I pull up alongside them.

'Hi!'

'Oh, hi Adam!'

They all turn round and smile at me. No, that's wrong. It's not that they smile at me, exactly. Their faces have already got smiles on them and they just swivel them in my direction.

'How's it going?'

'Wonderful!' They all say this together, like they're in a play or something. And I suddenly realise they all *look* the same. I mean, obviously, Natalie's got dark hair and glasses and Claire's got fair hair and no glasses and Shushmita's Asian, but their expressions are exactly the same.

'Isn't it a beautiful day?'

'Is this your little sister? She's beautiful!'

'Your car's beautiful, too!'

'Thanks.'

I can't think of anything else to say after this. I suppose I ought to ask Claire if she wants to go out tonight. I had been planning to be extra nice to her, to make up for all my shenanigans. (Even though she doesn't know about them.) But now I just don't feel like going out with her tonight. I know she'll be just as happy if we don't go out as if we do. That smile's not going anywhere.

I'm like, 'OK, catch you later.'

As I drive off down the road, I can see them in my mirror, standing there, smiling after me and waving.

I come up to Baker's Arms in Leyton. In case you don't know it, it's a busy crossroads with crap traffic lights. Whichever road you're coming up, and whether you're driving or walking, the lights always seem to be red. Normally you get quite a lot of horns beeping and people scowling and swearing at each other here. But today, of course, everyone's smiling. The drivers are all sitting back comfortably with their elbows sticking out the windows. Even though the traffic's even worse than usual today. As I get nearer, I can see why. There's been an accident.

A guy's lying in the road with his trousers soaked in blood. The car that hit him has stopped right in the middle of the junction. An ambulance has arrived and two ambulance guys are just about to load him on a stretcher.

I'm like, 'Don't look, Emily.'

I don't want her to see this. But it's too late, she's already seen it. And she's smiling, like some demonic kid in a horror film.

'That man's been runned over!'

'Yeah, poor guy.'

'He doesn't mind!'

And then I see that the guy's smiling too. So are the ambulance workers. And so is the driver of the car that hit him. He's standing there smoking a fag and grinning all over his face.

'Here you are,' he goes to the guy whose legs he's just crushed. 'Have a fag.'

'Thanks, mate,' goes the guy on the ground. 'I like a nice fag.'

'These fags are the best,' goes the driver. 'They're Benson's.'

'Yeah, you can't beat a Benny,' goes the guy on the ground.

'How are you? In any pain?' goes one of the ambulance men.

'Yeah, quite a lot of pain,' goes the guy, smiling and puffing on his fag. 'It's pretty bad. Intense pain.'

'Looks like you've lost a lot of blood,' goes the other ambulance man. 'You're gonna need a transfusion, you are.'

'Am I?'

'Yeah, without a blood transfusion you'll be dead in a few minutes.'

'Blimey!' goes the guy on the ground, and they all laugh.

I've had enough of this.

First I'm like, 'I wish the guy's legs were OK.'

The guy stands up. 'Hey, my legs are OK again!' He's still smiling in exactly the same way as when his legs were all mangled.

'Nice one,' says the first ambulance man.

'Sorted,' goes the second. 'No need for that blood transfusion after all!'

'Saves you a job then!'

And again they all laugh.

Then I'm like, 'I wish people would stop being happy all the time.'

And nothing happens.

They all carry on smiling just like before.

'Didn't you hear? I said I wish people would stop being happy!'

Still nothing happens.

I look round at Emily. She's smiling all over her face.

'Emily? How do you feel?'

'As happy as a watering-can!'

I get a sort of sinking feeling.

Something's gone badly wrong here.

'Genie! I wish you were here right now!'

I'm back home in my bedroom now. I couldn't stand seeing Emily smiling any more, so I put her to bed and wished her to sleep for a bit.

So, then there's this puff of smoke in the middle of the room, and it turns into a massive column of black smoke, then it solidifies into the genie, with his turban and his curled-up moustache and his purple silk trousers and his turned-up shoes. Like before, he's floating just a few centimetres off the floor.

'You sent for me. What is your wish?'

'I just made a wish and it didn't come true. What's going on? You said I had an infinite amount of wishes!'

'And so you have. Any wish you make will certainly be granted – as long as it is not logically contradictory.'

'Maybe you'd better explain that – logically contradictory. I can't see how I've wished for anything logically contradictory.'

'No wish can be granted if it is not within the rules of logic. If you wished for a four-sided triangle, that wish could not be granted. For no triangle could ever have four sides.'

'Yeah, I get that, but I didn't wish for a four-sided triangle, did I? I wished people would stop being happy. There's nothing contradictory about that.'

'There is, taken in conjunction with your earlier wish. For you wished that everyone would be happy for the rest of their lives. Now you wish that everyone is not happy for the rest of their lives. But people cannot be both happy for the rest of their lives and not happy for the rest of their lives.'

'That can't be right! Look, I wished Bobbligrubs could talk and then I wished he couldn't talk. That wasn't a problem!'

'You did not wish that Bobbligrubs could talk for the rest of his life. Had you done so, you would have found it impossible to unwish. If you impose a time condition on the wish, that is part of the wish. And it must be observed.'

'OK, OK. Look, there's gotta be some way round this. What should I wish to put it right?'

'There is nothing you can wish to put it right.'

I heard the words, but they didn't quite register yet. I didn't understand their finality.

'Come on, Genie! Gimme a break here. I can't put up with everyone grinning like Barbie and Ken all the time! It'd be a nightmare. Just help me out, will you?'

The genie folded his arms across his massive chest. 'I am sorry. There is nothing I can do.'

But he doesn't sound sorry at all. He sounds pretty smug, like he's just won an argument.

A spider of dread starts to scuttle through my guts.

'Please, genie!' My voice has a desperate ring to it now.

'I am sorry. There is nothing I can do.'

For a minute or two, I'm just, like, lost for words. I just stare at the guy. He's telling me I've got to live the rest of my life surrounded by grinning androids. Sixty or seventy years of it. Of course, *they* won't mind. *They'll* be all right. As far as they're concerned, they might as well be stuck in that Experience Machine Dirk was going on about. But what about me? I'll be the only normal guy left in the world. I'll go mad. I'll go crazy. I'll go insane.

'Genie, please! You gotta help me!'

'I am sorry. There is nothing I can do.'

I'm like, 'I wish I'd never met you!'

'I cannot grant that wish either, for that too is logically contradictory. If you had never met me, you would not now be in a position to –'

'I wish you'd just bugger off, then! That's not logically contradictory, is it?'

The genie smiles. 'No, that is not logically contradictory.'

He gets fuzzy round the edges. He turns back into a column of black smoke. The column of smoke gets smaller and smaller and then disappears.

And I'm left all alone.

I sat down heavily on the bed. I had an extremely serious problem here and it needed an extremely serious think.

As far as I could make out, there were only two options.

One, I could put up with everyone being constantly happy around me for the rest of my life. I'd never see anyone scowl again, or frown, or pout, or sulk, never hear anyone moan or grumble or say 'Ouch', never hear anyone swear or cry. Emily, for instance – she'd never cry, never, ever again. It seemed sort of like a deprived childhood, in a way, not being able to cry. Well, you may think, if she's happy, so what? The trouble was, it wasn't *real* – it was an artificial happiness that had nothing to do with what happened to her.

And the same for everyone else. I mean, it had nothing to do with life, you know? I could give someone a kiss or a kick up the arse and they'd be just as happy either way. It just didn't matter what people did any more.

In fact, I began to wonder how long people would stay alive under these conditions. Their lives might turn out to be pretty short. Because there was no reason people wouldn't just walk straight out into the traffic, now – they'd be just as happy getting run over as not getting run over. And if they got ill, there'd be no reason to go to the doctor, cause they'd be just as happy ill as if they got better. There was no reason for people to even eat any more. They'd be just as happy starving to death as scoffing their lunch.

Anyway, that was Option One. I didn't really like the sound of it. That left Option Two.

Option Two, right, was to wish to be happy for the rest of my life myself. Like everyone else. If you can't beat 'em, join 'em sort of thing. If I did that, at least I definitely would be happy.

Or *someone* would. But would it really still be me? Did I really want to turn myself into one of those grinning Barbie-and-Ken lookalikes? Smiling whatever happened to me? Grinning if a car knocked me over? Just as happy to have toothache as to have sex?

No. I didn't wanna do that.

I definitely did not want to do that.

No way.

If I never got pissed off, never got angry or frustrated, never had any ambitions or regrets – well, I just wouldn't be *me* any more, would I? I might as well be a happy little bee, or beetle, as a human being.

So that put me back to Option One again. I'd just have to live here in this crappy happy world, the only normal human being left on the planet.

Well, great. Wasn't that just fine and dandy. How had I done it? How had I managed to screw up so totally, with an infinite number of wishes to play with?

It was worse than those idiots in the story when the guy wished for a sausage and then his wife got really angry with him for wasting the wish and wished the sausage was stuck to his nose, and then they couldn't get it off and had to use the last wish to unstick it. All right, they wasted their wishes, but at the end of the day at least they still had the sausage. But look at me, what had I done? I'd made everyone in the world permanently off their faces with happiness – *except me.*

So, Option One was impossible and Option Two was unbearable.

Fine.

Great.

Well done, Adam.

I suddenly had this kind of vision of an awards ceremony for the biggest disasters in history – like the Oscars, with a shedload of celebs in dinner jackets and evening gowns sitting round tables and a babe on the stage with an envelope.

'The nominees are: Lord Cardigan for the Charge of the Light Brigade; the Captain of the Titanic for sinking the unsinkable; and Adam Gowers for turning everyone on the planet into a grinning android for the rest of their lives, except himself. And the winner is...' (tears open the envelope) '...Adam Gowers!'

The front door opened and I heard my dad come in, singing 'Zip-a-Dee-Doo-Dah' in that annoying, warbling voice of his.

No, I just couldn't hack it. It was... too much. But what was I going to do? I couldn't stand to wish myself into a permanent happy trance like everyone else. It'd be like wishing myself into, what's that ride at Alton Towers called, Oblivion, that's it. But at the same time, I couldn't stand another seventy years on this planet, surrounded by...

Wait a minute.

On *this* planet.

But I didn't have to stay on this planet, did I? With an infinite number of wishes I could go wherever I wanted.

The moon, Venus, Mars, the stars.

And let's face it, no one down here was going to miss me. They'd still be as happy as pigs in shit if they never saw me again for the rest of their lives.

I went into Emily's room. 'Bye, Em,' I said, in a hushed kind of voice. I didn't want to wake her. She looked so cute lying there with her hair over her cheek and her lips curved in a smile, I could almost pretend she was her old self again.

I went downstairs. Dad was in the kitchen making coffee.

'Hello Adam! What a wonderful lesson I've just had with Mrs Sprocket! Would you like a cup of this delicious coffee made with Fairtrade beans, all the way from Colombia?'

'No thanks, Dad. Look, I'm off on a journey. I may be gone some time.'

'Really? Where are you going?'

'I thought I might go to Outer Space.'

'Really? How extraordinary! How are you going to get there?'

'I'm gonna fly.'

'Amazing!'

'Yeah, look, give my love to Mum, OK?'

'I'll certainly do that!'

'Cool. Well, bye then.'

'Cheerio!'

I went out into the garden. I looked up at the sky. It was still cloudy, but there was a hole of blue in the clouds. It looked like a sort of window of hope, if you know what I mean. That was where I was going to aim for.

I was like, 'I wish I could fly straight up.'

My feet lifted off the ground. The lawn fell away beneath me.

Looking down, I saw my dad smiling and waving to me through the kitchen window.

CHAPTER 12

I rose up fast. The gap in the clouds was like this brilliant, glowing blue. It looked small from the ground – just enough to patch a sailor's trousers, as my mum says – but when I got nearer I saw it was big, the size of a football field. Enough to patch the trousers of the whole Royal Navy.

I passed through and rose above the clouds. They spread out for miles and miles all around me, shining all silver in the sun. It was pretty spectacular.

It was starting to get cold, though. I've never understood why it's colder higher up. I mean, why do mountains have snow on the top? You'd think it'd be warmer cause it's nearer the sun. Anyhow, it wasn't warm, it was bloody freezing. I was like, 'I wish I was nice and warm,' through chattering teeth.

A warm glow swept through my body. That was nice. But now I had another problem. I could hardly breathe. I kept sucking in great lungfuls of air, but it made no difference. The air wasn't like proper air up here. It was all thin and wispy. It was like, if you bit into candy floss expecting it to be solid, you'd get a sort of disappointed feeling in your mouth when you realised the stuff had no body to it. That was what this air was like. No body. Compared to real air, it was candyfloss. Except it wasn't sweet.

I'm like, 'I wish I could breathe properly,' and now, at last, I'm comfortable. I'm able to look round and appreciate the view. The clouds go rolling on and on beneath me, like another country up in the sky. I can see a couple of planes going by, with their wings glinting in the sunlight. Full of happy smiley passengers saying the in-flight movie is totally amazing and the airline food is the finest food they've ever tasted, no doubt. Far below, through gaps in the clouds, I can see glimpses of England and what looks like the sea. But I'd like to get a better view, so I wish that the clouds would part, and they do, they just roll away. Then I can see all of southern England, it's a sort of greeny-brown, and a blue-grey sea, and the coast of France. It's amazing, just like you see in atlases and stuff. I make a wish to rise faster. The Earth drops away. Now I can see all of Britain and France, and there's Ireland, and I'm high enough to see that the Earth is curved, it really is a great big ball, just like they say. It looks just like the globe we used to have in primary school. And it makes me think how amazing those guys were who worked out the shape of all the countries and sussed that the world was round and every-thing, without ever having the chance to fly up in the sky and take a proper look, but somehow they got it completely right. I mean, what an amazingly clever species we are.

Or were. Because everyone's too happy to be clever now and no one's ever going to make any more discoveries, ever again. And it's all my fault. Right. I know. Well, look, anyone can make a mistake, OK?

Though it's true that my mistake was a pretty uniquely awe-somely mega-colossal one.

And still I rise. That was the title of some book we did in English with Miss Rogers in Year 10, but I can't remember much about it. Poems, it was. I think some of them were quite good. Now I can see all of Europe and I can just see where it starts to get all white up at the top. That must be where the Arctic Circle begins, in the north of Sweden and Finland and those places. I make a wish to rise even faster.

I shoot up into the sky – but no, it doesn't feel like shooting up into the sky any more, I've lost my concept of sky. I'm shooting *away* from the Earth, into space. Down below I can see one whole side of the Earth now, Europe, Africa, the Atlantic, a bit of Asia. I look above me and I see it's all black. I must have left the atmosphere now. I can still breathe, though, cause of my wish.

The blackness is spangled with stars. They look much brighter than on Earth. They don't twinkle up here. They're just steady points of bright light. And I can visit any of them I like. It's kind of a weird thought.

So, where should I go? I decide I quite fancy the idea of going to visit Venus. I don't know why, I don't know much about it, but it sounds kind of nice – a planet named after the goddess of love. I haven't got a clue which of these points of light is Venus, of course, but that doesn't matter. I'm like, 'I wish to go to Venus, and step on it.'

Venus isn't all it's cracked up to be, I can tell you that for nothing.

You might expect it to be a beautiful planet, considering it's named after a beautiful goddess. Well, it's not beautiful in the slightest. In fact, you wouldn't be far wrong in calling it a shithole.

I went whooshing through space at incredible speed and suddenly there it was. Venus, looming up at me. I was only a little way above it – I say a little way, but it was probably a few thousand miles. It looked as big as – well, as big as a planet. It was a sort of bright brown in colour, if you can have bright brown, and you could see all these clouds sort of whirling round it. It was spectacular, but it also looked kind of scary. I was dropping down towards it at an amazing speed and I suddenly got this idea that it might not be totally safe. I'd already wished to be warm enough and to be able to breathe, but I got this feeling that that may not quite be enough, so I made another wish, 'I wish that I'm gonna be totally safe on this planet.'

It was a good job I did. As I plunged down into the layer of cloud I felt a stinging pain all over my body. Not enough to really hurt me, because of my wish, but enough to make me realise there was something more than a bit dodgy about these clouds. They gave off this terrible stink, it burned the inside of your nose. I wished I knew what they were made of, and the answer popped into my head – sulphuric acid. Well, I mean, great. What a way to welcome visitors.

I couldn't see a thing, just this thick reddish-brown mist – no, it was thicker than mist, it was more like a kind of soup. As I got closer to the surface I could feel the atmosphere pressing in on me more and more, like squashing me. If it hadn't been for my wish I'd have been as flat as a pancake. Also, it was getting hotter. And hotter. It was like falling down into a giant oven.

Suddenly, I was through the clouds. Below me was the surface of Venus. It looked like this huge brownish desert of rock – pretty flat, just a few hills, nothing much. There was no water to be seen, no trees, no sign of life anywhere. I was totally uncomfortable now – way too hot, and I had this feeling of being crushed by the atmosphere, and these stinging raindrops of sulphuric acid kept falling on my head. You wouldn't have liked it.

I landed on the surface with a bump. The rock was so hot I felt it burn up through the soles of my feet all the way up to my scalp. If it hadn't been for my wish I'd have been scorched to a cinder on the spot.

Just out of interest, I wished I knew how hot it was, so if I ever wrote postcards to the folks back on Earth I'd be able to tell them. The answer jumped into my head: *480 degrees Celsius.*

480 degrees!

What the hell was I doing in this place?

It was like… well, it was like hell.

I didn't hang around to explore. There was nothing to explore anyway, just miles and miles of baking red-hot rock. I just wished to be out of there, like immediately.

A moment later, I was floating around in the coolness of space, looking down at Venus raging away below me. Jesus, what a shit-hole. It made me realise how fantastic Earth was, with all its oceans and forests and fields and rivers and stuff. Compared to Venus, Earth was a babe. A stunner. Put it this way, if you were a bloke planet out on the pull, you'd hit on Earth every time, no question. You'd have to be out of your mind to even go near Venus.

Well, I zoomed along through space for a bit. What was I going to do next? I had thought of visiting Jupiter, cause I'd heard it was really big, and I liked the idea of going somewhere totally gigantic. But I'd gone off the idea now. Venus had put me off. It wasn't just the discomfort. There's something kind of *lonely* about visiting an empty planet.

There's something lonely about space, too. I looked at the blackness all around, speckled with tiny bright stars, millions and billions of miles away from me. OK, it was spectacular. But in a cold, icy, unfriendly, unwelcoming sort of way. There was something funny about it, and then I realised what it was. It was totally silent. I mean, completely 100% silent. On Earth, even when it's dead quiet, you can always hear something, maybe a bird singing, or a car in the distance, or just the wind. But up here, nothing. Not a peep.

I shivered, and not cause of the cold. I felt like I was going off space. It was too big. And too empty. And too lonely. And too quiet.

It was time to make a wish.

CHAPTER 13

I'm on another planet now. I don't know what it's called. I just wished to go to an empty planet. There's no life here. Except for me. I wanted somewhere to think.

It's cold. The sky is grey. There are mountains in the distance. I'm sitting on this long brown rock next to a frozen lake. There's a thin layer of snow on the ground. The only movement is the steam coming out my nostrils when I breathe. It goes straight up. The air is as still as, well, as still as a frozen lake.

Well, what am I going to do? I could set off and explore the universe, I suppose. Meet some alien life forms. If there are any. But what's the point? I don't want to meet alien life forms. Not right now. I'm not in the mood. I want to be back on Earth, with the people I know. Playing with Emily, having a laugh with Dirk, going out with Claire.

But I can't go back to Earth. I can't face all those grinning androids who used to be people I knew. Poor little Emily, I miss her. I wonder how far away she is. Millions of light years, I suppose. I'm all on my own, millions of light years away from home. It's lonely up here. It's crap. It's worse than crap. It's hell. I thought Venus was bad, but this is worse. And it's not going to get any better, is it?

How am I going to get by? Frankly I don't think I am going to get by. This has all got a bit too much for me. I don't know what I'm going to do next.

I'm at rock bottom. And my bottom is on a rock. Hmm, that's a kind of joke, isn't it?

Not a very funny one, though.

I don't know how long I sat there, thinking like this. A couple of days, I reckon, cause I seem to remember it got dark and then light and then dark and then light again. But that doesn't tell me much, because I don't know how long the days are on this planet. All I know is, after a time, it seemed like I couldn't sit there thinking these thoughts any more.

I mean, I just couldn't stand it.

I opened my mouth and some words came out.

'I wish I was dead.'

And nothing happened.

'Didn't you hear? I said I wish I was dead!'

Still nothing happened.

'Right, genie! I wish you were here right now!'

A puff of black smoke, and there he is, with his turban and his moustache and his turned-up shoes.

'Yes?'

'Look, genie, I just wished to be dead and I'm still alive. How do you explain that?'

'No wish that is logically contradictory may be granted.'

'Yeah, yeah, I know that. But what's logically contradictory about being dead?'

'You wished for an infinite number of wishes. Therefore you must have an infinite number of wishes.'

'Wodjer mean?'

'If you were to die now, you would not be able to make any more wishes. You would not have fulfilled your wish.'

I started to feel sick. 'What are you saying? How many wishes have I gotta make before I can die, then?'

'An infinite number.'

'But I'll *never* get to an infinite number of wishes!'

'Precisely.'

I just stared at the guy for a bit, hoping he was joking.

He didn't crack a smile.

I'd got to be a bit of a specialist in sinking feelings recently, but this one was something else. It wasn't so much a sinking feeling as a plummeting feeling. I felt like I'd just stepped over a cliff, or down a lift shaft, or jumped out of a plane and pulled the ripcord on my parachute and the fucking thing hadn't opened. I was plunging down, down, down and there was no way back up.

'So – what are you saying? That – that I can never die?'

'Precisely.'

'What – you're saying I'm immortal?'

'Precisely.'

'But I don't *wanna* be immortal!'

'I am sorry to hear that.'

'Well – what can I do about it?'

'There is nothing you can do about it.'

I didn't say anything for about five minutes. Then I was like, 'Well, isn't that just great.'

Then I didn't say anything for another five minutes.

Then I was like, 'All right, genie. You might as well bugger off again.'

He disappeared, leaving me alone on my long brown rock.

Again, I don't know how long I sat there. Time passed. At some point I got hungry and wished for a pizza. One with pepperoni and asparagus on. And another time I wished for some fish and chips. And some time later I wished for a chicken tikka masala. And for a flushing toilet. With a heated seat, and quilted toilet paper. Might as well be comfortable.

Apart from that I didn't say or do anything for – well, several days, probably. I was wondering how I was going to take an eternity of this. You can't eat chips and pizza and curry for all eternity. Well, you could, but it's going to get pretty boring. *Everything's* going to get boring. Eternity, eternity, eternity.

Just think about it. Everything else will end. But I'll go on. Stars will burn out, planets will be consumed in their fires. One day, maybe in about ten billion years, the whole universe will have run down. There'll be nothing, just blackness and coldness forever and ever and ever. And me, floating around in space all on my own. And suicide not even an option.

Maybe I'll find a way out of this universe. Through a black hole. The black hole would crush me but it couldn't kill me and I'd come out the other side into another universe. Maybe.

But then what?

I'd still be confronted by *eternity.*

I reckon that genie cheated me. He should have warned me right at the beginning, back there in the attic. Don't have anything to do with genies, that's my advice. You can't trust them.

It's fair to say I was kind of depressed.

But there came a time when I couldn't stand sitting there doing nothing any more.

I decided to liven the view up a bit. I wished for some trees.

That was nice. Then I wished for some birds singing in the branches. That was nice too.

So, right, what else could I wish for to while away eternity?

And then I had an idea. Like a really simple one. I don't know why I didn't think of it before. It was staring me in the face.

'I wish I could think of something to make life worth living.'

And suddenly my brain moved into high gear!

I opened my mouth and made my wish.

PART THREE: HOW IT CARRIED ON AFTER THAT

CHAPTER 14

The torch on my phone lit up cardboard boxes, an old vacuum cleaner, a rocking-horse, the water tank, an old rug and a portrait of a sad-looking babe with a harp. It was nice and warm up in the attic, after sitting on that cold bare rock by that frozen lake on that godforsaken planet.

I could hear my mum downstairs telling Emily not to eat the newspaper and I could hear my dad pottering about with the car on the drive, and I could hear Bobbligrubs barking out in the garden.

I just stood there, listening and savouring it for a bit, feeling the house around me like an old coat or something. I was home. It was cool.

Life was worth living again.

It took a long and complicated wish to bring me here. Well, a whole series of wishes, really. This is what I wished, up on that horrible lonely planet:

'Right, genie, are you listening? I wish this planet was exactly the same size and shape as Earth. And I wish it had exactly the same climate. I wish it had a moon that looked exactly the same and was the same distance away as the old one. And I wish it had a sun just like the old one too, same size, same temperature, same distance away, and a solar system of identical planets, OK? And I wish when you looked up in the sky at night you saw all the same stars as on Earth. I wish the geography here was the same as on Earth too – all the same continents, same seas, same mountains and rivers and deserts and forests and all that stuff, OK? And all the same villages and towns and cities. And all the same species of animals and the same numbers of them.

'Right, now, the people. This is very important. I want there to be exactly the same number of people on this planet as there were on Earth just before I made my first wish. And I want them all to be the same ages as they were on Earth. And I want them all to have the same names as they had on Earth. And I want them all to

165

look exactly the same – and they've got to *be* exactly the same. I don't want them to be just, like, robots, I wish that they're the same inside as they were on Earth – with the same consciousness, the same memories, same likes and dislikes, same imaginations, same abilities, same values and beliefs, same good and bad qualities and all that stuff. There's got to be an Emily and a Dirk and a Claire and a Natalie and an everyone, even a Steve Renwick, and they've got to be exactly the same as the ones I knew on Earth – like, exact replicas, you know, but they've got to be real people. Same DNA. Like clones, but they mustn't know they're clones.

'Now, I wish I was in an exact replica of my old house – everyone's house has got to be exactly the same as it was, OK – and I wish I was up in the attic, just like I was on the day I met you. And I wish it was the same date, Saturday February 12th. And I wish I was the same as I was then, too, OK?'

That was the wish that brought me back home – or brought home back to me, I suppose. It's kind of hard to get your head round, isn't it? Like, you, yes, *you* reading this, you're one of the replicas I created. You can't tell the difference, of course, that's the whole point of the wish. But your original self, if it's still alive, is grinning away like an android that's been programmed to be happy, back on the original Earth.

I shone my torch around a bit. I could just see the genie's lamp peeping out behind the picture of the sad-looking bird with the harp, but I left it alone. Now, what had I come up here for? Dad's old tennis racket, that was it.

There it was. An old wooden racket, with the paint peeling off it. It was encased in one of those old racket press things, you know, a kind of square wooden frame that's supposed to stop it from warping. I unscrewed the press and took it out and swung it around a bit. The racket, I mean, not the press. So, I was ready for my game of tennis with Natalie, now. I'd send her the Valentine card and…

I stopped swinging the racket.

Wait a minute.

Who was I trying to kid? What was the *point* in sending her a Valentine or challenging her to a game of tennis?

She didn't fancy me. I'd had that demonstrated with blinding clarity. I heard it from her own lips when I was a fly on the wall. What more proof did I need? She fancied Dirk. Why not let her have him? (Maybe that was hard on Shushmita, but she still had Kiss My Chuddies.)

Plus, I wasn't even sure if I fancied Natalie any more. I was worn out with it. Knackered. Exhausted, you know, with not being appreciated. She didn't even laugh at my jokes. She'd be better off with Dirk. They could talk about philosophy and Emily Bronte and other highbrow subjects together.

I dropped the racket. It fell next to a pair of ancient blue flippers. You couldn't wear them to a swimming pool or anything. You'd be a laughing stock. But they gave me an idea.

What about Claire? Why not send the Valentine card to Claire?

I

would
love
to go swimming with
you.

Claire likes swimming.

And she likes me.

And I like her.

She laughs at my jokes. She said I was gorgeous. Though that was after I'd had my appearance changed. Maybe she won't think I'm gorgeous now I'm my old self again. But... maybe she will. Going swimming's a cool idea, cause I'll get the chance to see her in a swimming costume. Course, I've seen her in a lot less than that. But not in this world. I suddenly realise I haven't been to bed with her, not in this world. In this world, we're both still virgins, in a way. It's kind of an exciting prospect. I can feel a sort of warm stirring in the region. Claire is the one for me!

And I didn't realise it when she was my girlfriend. Stupid tosser! I'm the stupid tosser, I mean, not her. But this time – if I get the chance – we're going to be great together. We never got round to having that conversation about comics I wanted to have with her, I realise. I'm looking forward to that. And maybe if I practised the piano more, we could play duets together, with her on the violin. We could start with 'The Trout'. At least I know the first half of it.

I'm going to make it work this time.

I really am.

There's just one thing. My wishes.

I want to make it happen without wishes. That won't be easy. I know from experience that if you've got wishes, you can't help using them.

And then I get another idea. And I act on it fast, like without delay. Cause I know if I hesitate I'll have second thoughts and then I won't do it.

So before I have a chance to stop myself, I just blurt it out.

'I wish I couldn't use my wishes for the next seventy years.'

There.

Done it.

I don't feel any different after this wish, so just to check it I go, 'I wish for a sausage sandwich.'

Nothing happens.

So, that's it, then. I'm back in the land of the normal. It's kind of scary. But I'm glad to be back. Life's exciting again! It's full of uncertainty! I can't control events any more. I've got to deal with them.

Of course, there's still a problem. All I've done is postpone it, really. When I'm 87, I'll get my wishes back, and what will I do then? Wish to be young again? Wish everyone who's died is alive again? Change planets? I'll still have eternity to sort out. Eternity's not going to go away.

But… that's OK. I feel optimistic now. I've got plenty of time to think of something.

In the meantime, I've got plenty of stuff to keep me busy. Like I've got a fight booked with that psycho Steve Renwick on Monday. Got to deal with it somehow. And my AS levels coming up in the summer. Got to deal with them. And my bitter, bickering, wine-glugging parents. Got to deal with them. And getting zits again.

Got to deal with it. And being crap at economics again and enduring Tubby's pathetic sarcasm. Got to deal with it. And being crap at football again. Got to deal with it. And being crap at playing the piano cause I never practise. Got to deal with it.

And asking Claire out and not knowing if she'll say yes...

But I've got a good feeling about that. I reckon she'll say yes. But what if she doesn't say yes? But I've got a feeling she will.

But what if I'm wrong?

But I'm hoping I'm right...

My mobile goes off.

I look at the caller's name.

It's Claire.

Patrons

Charleen Adams
Noga Applebaum
Leila Baker
Jago Barge
Annabelle Barnes
Andrew Cole
Toby Darling
Rebecca de Quin
Jenny Doughty
Daniel Fishel
Beth Gordon
Wim Hentenaar
Sally Howard
Steve Howie
Fran Hunter
Joachim Magens
Susanne Mathies
Carlo Navato
Polly Polly Russell
Christian Robshaw
Frederick Robshaw
Doug Shearer
Deborah Smith
John Sparrowhawk
Susie Steiner
Jo Symmons
Hugh Yeaman
Tamar Yoseloff